Annie Slosson

Dumb Foxglove, and other Stories

Annie Slosson

Dumb Foxglove, and other Stories

ISBN/EAN: 9783743348851

Manufactured in Europe, USA, Canada, Australia, Japa

Cover: Foto ©Andreas Hilbeck / pixelio.de

Manufactured and distributed by brebook publishing software (www.brebook.com)

Annie Slosson

Dumb Foxglove, and other Stories

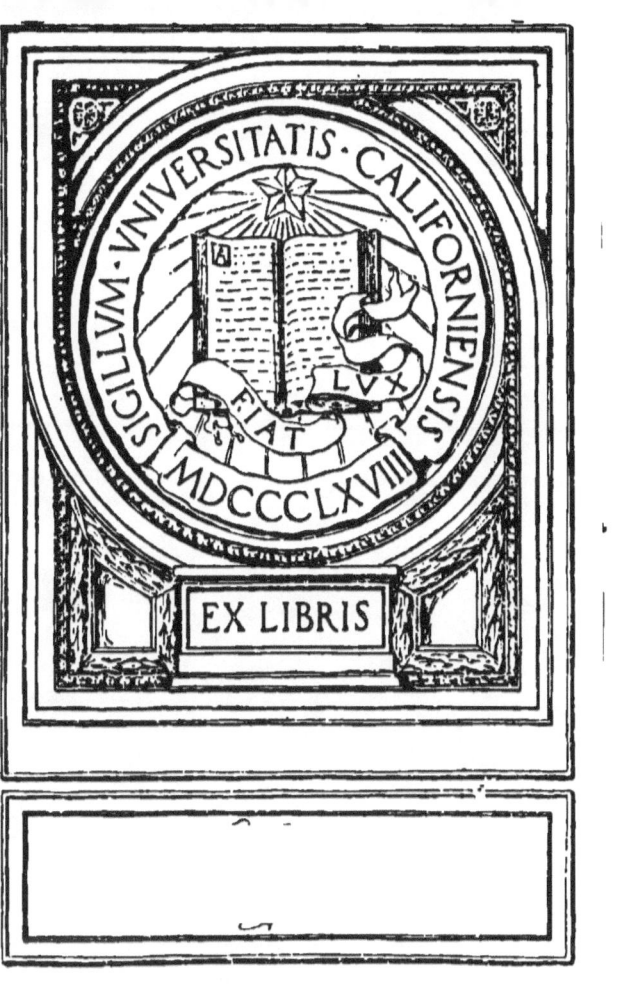

SIGILLVM · VNIVERSITATIS · CALIFORNIENSIS

FIAT LVX

MDCCCLXVIII

EX LIBRIS

DUMB FOXGLOVE

and

Other Stories

BY

ANNIE TRUMBULL SLOSSON

AUTHOR OF "SEVEN DREAMERS"
"FISHIN' JIMMY" ETC.

NEW YORK AND LONDON
HARPER & BROTHERS PUBLISHERS
1898

CONTENTS

DUMB FOXGLOVE

DUMB FOXGLOVE

ALL the golden October day we had been driving leisurely along through the Green Mountain country.

Everything was golden that fall. It had been a very dry season, and the leaves upon the maples and other forest trees, instead of ripening into brilliant hues of crimson and scarlet, had all taken on tints of yellow. Then, when the autumn winds arose, suddenly the whole earth was carpeted with saffron, daffodil, amber, and gold, a thick, soft, rustling carpet, and for days our horses trod upon it, and our wagon-wheels rolled over and through it. Somehow it had the effect of sunshine, and even in cloudy weather we were in the light. But the sun shone that day, and the air was soft and warm. There had been as yet no heavy frost, and the late flowers were still bright, while berry, seed-vessel, and nut were gay with red, blue, rus-set, and gold.

Goldenrod was massed by the road-side in tints to match every shade of our leafy car-pet, making for it a gorgeous border of gold color, and asters contrasted or harmonized, with their hues of mauve, blue, purple, lav-ender, and white.

The twisted orchid, or lady's-tresses, with its spike of frosted white bells, smelling of bitter almonds, clustered thickly in damp spots along the road-side; Joe Pye weed, or pink boneset, stood stiffly erect, with flat-topped clusters of dull-pink feathery blos-soms, and sometimes a belated St.-John's-wort added its yellow to the prevailing brightness. The witch-hazel bore on leafless brown boughs its strange flowers of straw color with their sickly sweet odor; and, most abundant of all, grew, all along our way, the dark-blue closed gentian.

There were so many berries! The short, thick spike which jack-in-the-pulpit wears; the sapphire-blue bear-plums; those of trans-lucent garnet, growing like a bunch of ripe

currants on the little smilacina; the crimson fruit of twisted-stalk, hanging singly on
slender stems; the mountain-holly's rosy red;
moose-berries; bunch-berries; the red cohosh
and the white, the last like beads of white
enamel strung upon red coral stalks—all
these we saw and gathered ere the day ended.
We were climbing the steep turnpike road
which crosses the mountains from Manches-
ter to Landgrove and Chester, and we often
left the wagon to walk by its side or linger
behind it, in the soft air and warm sunshine.
We gathered armfuls of maidenhair and
ostrich-ferns, wild flowers, berries, moss, and
lichen. And many other things we brought
back to the wagon unknowingly; for hun-
dreds of seed-vessels, of varied forms, prick-
ly, bristly, sticky, barbed, or thorned, clung
to our garments, as we scrambled through
the tangle of plants and shrubs at the
road-side, or strayed into the forests on either
hand. The long, slender Spanish needles;
the two-thorned fruit of the yellow bur-
marigold; the agrimony seed-holders, looking like tiny green feather-dusters; the odd,
flat, thin joints of the tick-trefoil pods;

the small green burs of enchanter's night-shade—all these and scores of other fast-hold-ing, close-clinging, little hindering things cov-ered our clothing and pricked our fingers in our journey that day.

We were to spend the night at Peru, that quiet mountain village we knew so well, and among whose pleasant people we had many friends.

The bouquet we had gathered along the way was not a satisfactory one, and there was little of beauty about it when we reached our destination. The golden leaves, full of sunshine as they hung on the branches or lay in our pathway, were dried and shrivelled now ; the berries were crushed, or had fallen from their stems ; the asters looked forlorn, with their rays twisted and drooping. But the closed gentians were unchanged, and we carried into the house with us a big bunch of the strange, undeveloped, bud-like flowers of dark purple-blue. And it was the sight of these blossoms as they stood in the old cream-ware pitcher on the sideboard, that evening, that made Aunt Eunice—every one in Peru called her by that name—tell the story.

"Yes, I know it isn't its real name, but that's what I always call it myself. Ma used to call it that, and so I do. And it's a real good name, come to think of it—dumb fox-glove. For it's a good deal like the foxglove that grows in the garden, you know, and it's the dumbest flower, for a real full-growed one, that I know. Never opens out into real blowth, you see, and nothing can make it. Water or sunshine or rich soil, loosening the dirt round it, or transplanting, or anything, don't make any difference; it won't open out. But pick it open and there 'tis, just like the prettiest posy in the world, streaked and painted and all, and nobody ever seeing it. It's dreadful queer why it's that way, ain't it? If the pretty part's all inside and hid and shut up, and isn't ever to do any-body a mite of good, why, what's it made that way for? Why didn't they leave the inside just plain, not finished off any, sort of skimped that part, you know, that wasn't to show? But there! it isn't half so queer and puzzling about posies as 'tis about folks, is it, now? For you know as well as I do, don't you, there's lots of folks just that same way.

They're all shut up tight, all in the dark and cold and lonesomeness, and never showing the pretty part inside that most of them's got after all. I never see that dumb foxglove that I don't think of Colossy Bragg. She lived just down the road there, in the house with so much of that wild-cucumber vine running over it, and the marigold bed in front.

" David and Lucy Ann Bragg were married a good while before they had any children, and they were dreadful pleased when this one came. She was a nice, big baby, and they thought she was going to take after Grandma West, and be tall and fleshy and fine-looking. So they named her, out of a book, Colossa, but we called it — you know how they do with such names about here— Colossy. Poor child, it didn't turn out a very suitable name for her. She was a healthy, nice little thing, rugged as any child, till she was about four years old. Then something took her — the doctors never seemed to know what, exactly — and she stopped growing. Her legs and arms were helpless like, and she couldn't walk or use

8

her hands much. 'Twas the pitifulest sight to see her. Her mind was all right; it was only the poor, pinched-up, pindling body that was wrong.

"Her face was real pretty, sort of thin and white, but with such big, dark, purple-blue eyes, almost black by spells—they made me think lots of times of the color of those dumb foxgloves—and long, black eye-winkers curling up at the ends. And her hair was long and soft, and such a pretty yellow, and it curled all round her head. She used to sit all day in a big chair with pillows, by the southwest window there, and every one for miles round Peru knew that pretty white face. 'Twas terrible hard on her pa and ma, they'd set so much by her, and lotted so on what she'd be when she grew up. They learnt her to read, but that was about all. For she couldn't use her hands, so there wasn't any ciphering, or drawing pictures on her slate, or sewing patch-work, or any of the things girls did in those days. She never seemed to care much about story-books. To be sure, there wa'n't many in those times; not what young ones call story-books now-

9

adays, with red-and-gold covers and painted pictures and all. But there was a few in
the place, and folks was glad enough to lend
them to poor little Colossy.

"The Braggses owned *Pilgrim's Progress*
and *Evenings at Home* themselves, and I had
Anna Ross and *Dairyman's Daughter*. And
here and in Landgrove and about there was
Little Henry and His Bearer, and *The Shepherd of Salisbury Plain*, and some numbers
of the *Juvenile Miscellany*, and there was
some books about missionaries, and some
travels. She had them all, one after another,
and as long as she wanted them, but they
didn't interest her much. And there wasn't
many things she could play. Puss-in-the-
corner and tag and blind-man's-buff and
trisket-a-trasket and all such running-about
plays was out of the question, course, and
even checkers and tit-tat-toe and fox-and-
geese, and set-down games like those, she
couldn't play at on account of her poor, helpless hands. Why, she couldn't even put
down her mite of a forefinger with the other
children's and say, 'Hinty minty cuty corn,'
to see who was 'it,' as the youngsters used to

say. She had a kind of weak, whisp'ry voice, so she couldn't even sing; and she didn't appear to care much about hearing tunes, neither. So you see she was nigh as much shut up and blind and dumb a little creatur' as that flower there.

"You wouldn't have thought, when you saw her sitting in her high-chair, bolstered up with pillows, her little drawed-up hands all helpless in her lap, and a shawl wrapped round her poor feet and legs—you wouldn't have thought there was anything in the world to interest her or make her forget her troubles. But there was. There was just one thing that kept her up, occupied her mind, amused her all day long, and made her willing to live and be so different from the other children. How it came first into her head I don't know, for 'twas the very last thing you'd ever expect would 'a' got there, considering what she was, poor, rickety little mite.

"It was cooking! Now, o' course you know she couldn't cook with her own hands, little, limp, crooked things that they was, but some ways or other she'd got the greatest faculty for making up dishes. 'Twas all she really cared about, the only thing that made her little bleached-out face lighten up, and those queer, pretty, purply eyes shine a speck. She was all the everlasting time composing, as you might say. But it wasn't verses or stories she made up, but things to eat, victuals. Where she got it all, as I said before, I never could see. There wasn't anything like it in the family, either side, Braggses or Wests. Her folks liked good, plain, filling food, and plenty of it, and Colossy hadn't ever seen anything different. But from the time she was a mite of a young one she was always making up the most beautiful receipts, and laying out the most fixed-up, company-looking dishes. To this day I often think over some of the victuals she talked about, and I can't help wishing they could be tried; they'd make your mouth water, they sounded so good and tasty.

"But somehow you couldn't make them; there was always something or other to be put in that you couldn't get, even if you could afford it. And they were generally pretty expensive victuals, too. Real receipt-

books she didn't care much about. Her
mother had one all writ out nice, in a little
book made of ruled paper. It came from
Aunt Huldy West, her father's sister. And
it had real good receipts, too : baked Indian
pudding—the Wests was always great for
that—and crollers, and Aunt Jane's tea-rusk,
and hard gingerbread, and huckleberry holler, and composition cake, and lots of other
things. But Colossy didn't care to hear it
much. She'd get fidgety after a spell, when
her ma was reading it, and then 's soon as
she got a chance she'd begin something of
her own. Some of the ingredients, as the
cooking-books say, were the funniest things.
She'd come across them, I suppose, in stories
and newspapers, in the missionary books and
the travels, but most of all in the Bible. They
were queer, outlandish, foreign things, that
couldn't be bought round this part of the
world, if they could anywheres. But she'd
tell them off till you'd know, or think you
did, just how they tasted, and, what's more,
could see the whole thing dished up, too.

"It all comes back as I tell about it, and
I can 'most hear Colossy's croupy, hoarse

voice saying over those things. 'Take a
teacupful o' anise an' cummin,' she'd croak
out—'an' mind it's a blue chiny teacup, not
a plain white; put it into a yaller bakin'-
dish, an' pour on a pint o' milk an' honey.
Beat it all up till it's white an' bubbly and
soapsudsy, an' then add ten clusters o' raisins. Stir for an hour an' twelve 'n' a half
minutes by the settin'-room clock. Then
you chop up the peel o' nineteen rorangers'
—she always called them that—'an' mix into
the hull mess. An' then—now listen, Aunt
Eunice,' she'd say, so solemn an' old-fashioned, 'for this is the most partic'lerest thing
in it—bile five an' a half turtle-dove's eggs
kind o' hard, take off the shell, an' lay 'em
over the puddin'—for it's goin' to be a puddin' this time, Aunt Eunice—an' bake half
an hour in a quick oven.'

"'And what's the name of that?' I used to
ask, just to please her and show I was listening.

"'Well,' she says, slow, and stopping to
think a little, 'well, that's called jest a Plain,
Fam'ly Puddin'. But here's one for comp'-
ny,' says she. 'I made it up last night,

when I couldn't get to sleep, my back hurt so, and it's the very nicest puddin'—this is a puddin', too—you never, never eat; an' it's so sightly to look at, an' sets off the table so. Now listen, Aunt Eunice,' she says. 'It's called Comp'ny Puddin'. Take two pomygranites and crack 'em, an' pick out the meats careful. Chop 'em fine, an' sprinkle over 'em a pinch o' frankincense and a teenty, teenty speck o' myrrh. Wet it up with a little maple surrup. Then take some fresh bread-fruit an' toast a few slices brown; lay 'em on a green-spriggled chiny meat-dish, an' spread your pomygranite sass all over 'em. Then beat the whites of ten ostrich's eggs for an hour 'n' a half, an' lay over the hull; sprinkle with light-brown sugar, an' dish up hot. Oh, Aunt Eunice!' she'd say, with her little thin face working and such a pitiful look in her big eyes, 'I wish I could try it my own self. I know I could do it, an' oh, how I'd like to beat up them ostrich's eggs an' spread 'em over, all sudsy an' nice, an' then sprinkle that light-brown sugar on!'

"'What's pomygranites, Colossy?' I'd ask her, to divert her mind a little.

"'Why, it tells about 'em in the Bible,' she says, 'an' Mr. Interpreter give some to Christiana, in *Pilgrim's Progress.*'

"You know I said 'twas this cooking or making up dishes that helped her along, and kept her amused and occupied. Well, it did, one way; but another it made her uncomfortable, for she did want so bad to cook and bake and mix up things, to be over the fire, stirring and basting, and baking and boiling. She ached to set the table and dish up the victuals, and make things look as they did in her mind when she composed them. She never fretted because she couldn't play about with the boys and girls, or hoppity-skip along the road, or slide, or run, or jump rope. But she did worry a good deal because she couldn't carry out the things she had in her head, nor mix a single one of the sightly and tasty dishes she was always making up. 'Course I like to think about 'em,' she'd say in her husky voice, 'but lots o' times I think, What's the good of it, anyway? What's the use o' settin' here an' makin' up receipts for puddin's an' cake an' jells an' all, an' never try 'em, nor see 'em, nor taste the teentiest speck

on 'em? I'm tired settin' here, an' I'm tired
achin' an' keepin' still an'— Oh, I do jest
want to have a bakin'-day of my own, an' try
some o' them things !'

"'Twas pretty hard to know what to say
to her for comfort. She was a good little
thing, and she'd been trained right, for the
Braggses were pious, church-going folks, and
I really believe she was a Christian before
she was ten year old. But that didn't make
much difference as to the thing she was fretting about just then. 'Twasn't heaven and
singing and all the glorious things we know
there'll be there that the poor little thing
was achin' for those times, but just a mite of
fussing and messing and cooking before she
went away from this earth that was such a
lonesome place for her. So I used to be at
my wits' ends to know what to tell her to
comfort her up when she went on that way ;
and her pa and ma, they were just as bothered
as me. But there was one person that hadn't
any such scruples as we had, and sometimes
I was kind of glad there was. 'Twas old Mrs.
Peavy that lived next door—Mother Peavy,
as everybody called her. She was real old,

a good deal over seventy anyway in those days, and I don't know but she was a mite childish. But she was smart and spry for her age, and her eyesight and hearing were as good as ever. And she was a dreadful comfort to Colossy, that's certain. For, as I said before, she hadn't any scruples—that is, the kind the rest of us had. Maybe you'll think she was a heathen, or a heretic, or something of that sort, when I tell you what she used to say to the child; but I am sure she meant well, and it did seem to help Colossy lots.

"'Oh, Mother Peavy,' the young one would say, 'won't I never, never have no chance to try em? If I'm real good an' patient, an' say my prayers an' my catechis' an' my hymns, an' do 's I'd be done by, an' all, won't I, oh, won't I never be let to try a single one o' them receipts? Jest not even the b'iled dish, with coriander seeds for flav'rin', an' thickened up with fine flour mingled with ile? Oh, won't I, Mother Peavy?'

"'Yes, yes, you poor little cosset,' Mother Peavy 'd say; 'don't you worry an' fret over that. If you want to mess an' cook an' try receipts when you get up there, you'll be let to do it. An' you'll be able to then, you know, for you'll be strong an' well an' rugged; for there ain't a single inhabitant up there that ever says "I'm sick," an' there won't be any more pain. An' your poor little drawed-up fingers will be straight an' sound, an' your legs strong and limber. An' you'll lift up the hands that's a-hangin' down now, and the feeble knees, as the Bible says, an' then if you're set on cookin' an' dishin' up they'll let you try, you see if they don't.'

"'But, Mother Peavy,' Colossy 'd whisper in her hoarse, short-breathing way, 'be you certain sure they've got things to do with up there? There's harps, an' crowns, an' books to sing out on, an' a sea o' glass, an' golden streets, an' all them pretty, pretty things, but mebbe they don't have the kind o' things you'd oughter have for cookin' an' dishin' up. Mebbe it's bad to want 'em, Mother Peavy, but—oh, I jest do sometimes!'

"'No, 'tain't bad, you poor young one; they understand up there, an' they make 'lowances. That's what they're great at in that place, you know, makin' 'lowances; must be the principal thing they do, these times, any-

way. An' if they see they ain't no other
means o' settin' your poor little mind easy
an' showin' you there's more satisfyin', fillin'
things than victuals, why, they'll give you
your way an' let you try. An' as for there
not bein' any eatable things there, why, the
Bible tells about twelve kinds o' fruit, an'
about olive-trees an' oil an' wine. An' there's
that hymn you like so much, about

"'There cinnamon an' sugar grow,
There nard an' balm abound.'

Take my word for it, Colossy, there won't be
no lack o' things to do with, if you want 'em
bad.'

"An' the child would take a dreadful lot of
comfort out of all her talk, and always stop
fretting, at least for a spell.

"Now I know it wasn't right; we all knew
it. The way was to show her how much
better things there were than what she was
set on—spiritual food that she didn't dream
of, poor, stunted, shut-up little soul. But
Mother Peavy always made out that there
wasn't any harm in it; that she didn't really
say there would be cooking and dishing up

there, but only that if Colossy was still set on that kind of amusement after she got there, she'd be let to try it. 'But she won't want it then, you see,' she'd say. 'She'll have better work there, more satisfyin'. So it don't do any harm, an' it does go against me to see her fret, the dear lamb.'

"So they were great cronies, she and Colossy, and had long confabs together. 'Twas mighty queer talk to listen to, I can tell you, and you'd get all mixed up and confused to know whether 'twas real flesh-and-blood food of this world they was dwelling on, or the spiritual, heavenly sort. For 'twould be manna and milk and honey and angels' food and unleavened bread and balm of Gilead and all that, which might be just figurative or speaking parables like. But again 'twould be cakes and puddings and stews, with spices and oil and spikenard and leeks and onions and almonds and turtle-doves and melons, till your mouth watered.

"But it really beat all how much that child found about victuals in the Bible; things none of us ever knew was there till she brought them into her receipts. And then

we'd look them up and find they were really
there. And to this day I recollect them, and
time and again, as I come across them in
reading a chapter, I think of poor little Colossy and her talk : fish and summer fruit and
wheat and barley and millet and apples and
butter and broth and nuts and vinegar and
parched corn and grapes and raisins and figs
and—why, I can't tell half of them now.
Why, once, I know, she told about some dish
or other, and there was to be a pound of
pannag. We thought she'd made that up,
sure. But come to look it up, there 'twas in
Ezekiel, and there 'tis to this day, though I
haven't the least idea what 'tis or where it
comes from.

"Poor little creatur', she looked for that
kind of thing, and of course she found it.
There's everything folks want in that book.
And she got a good deal of a real different
sort of comfort out of it, too. She'd be turning over the leaves of the big Bible on the
table, as well as she could with her little
twisted bony fingers, looking for new 'ingre-
junts,' as she called them, for her dishes, and
you'd see such a pretty look come on her

white face. An' she'd draw a long breath, as if she was resting after a hard job, and look up with her big purply eyes all soft and wet, and say over something she'd found there. 'Twas something generally about getting rest, or casting your burdens off, or being carried or comforted as a mother comforteth, or having tears wiped away, or something like that. No, it was not all vict- uals she found there. But it's the victuals part of the story I'm telling you now.

"The minister that time was Mr. Robbins. He was a real good man, and terribly sorry for Colossy. He used to go and see her a good deal, and try to help her, and teach her, and raise her thoughts higher. But when she got on that favorite topic of hers, why, he didn't know just what to say. 'Twas a sight to see his face, after he'd been reading and talking and praying with her a spell, and she'd been so sweet and good, and seemed in such a promising state of mind, when she'd look up so pitiful just before he went away and croak out, 'Oh, Mr. Robbins, won't you jest listen to one single one o' my receipts now?'

"He generally did, for he was a good-natured man and had children of his own, but he'd try to put on a moral at the end and draw some kind of a lesson from it all. 'Now hear this, Mr. Robbins,' she says one time, speaking slow and plain as if she was reading from a receipt-book. 'Di-rec-tions for ma-king a mess of pottage.'

"'Yes, yes, my little girl,' he says, 'I'll hear it; but be careful lest you part with your own heavenly birthright for a mess of pottage,' he says.

"'Yes, sir,' says Colossy very quick, for she was in a hurry to go on with her receipt, 'I'll be careful. Take one fatted calf'—and on she'd go, till Mr. Robbins's face was just a picture, kind of puzzled, and sort of amused, too.

"Or she'd tell off a receipt for 'raising un-leavened bread,' poor little cosset, and the minister 'd remind her that 'man shall not live by bread alone.' Again 'twould be some sort of a savory meat stew, and he'd counsel her to labor not for the meat that perisheth. But he was always good and kind to the child, and she was real fond of him to the last.

"Poor little thing, she took it all out in making up and telling about victuals, for she hardly eat anything herself. Whether it was her made-up, make-believe dishes was so good it took away her taste for common, every-day food, I don't know, but she didn't eat enough to keep a robin alive, and so, of course, she didn't get very strong or rugged. Fact is, you couldn't want her to stay on here, suffering and shut up and helpless as she was, and as she'd got to be all her days. And we all saw pretty soon that she wasn't going to be here much longer. Her little scrap of a face got thinner and whiter, and the purple eyes bigger, and the little hands more than ever like bird's claws; and her poor little body was wasted away and weak. She was real patient, but the ache in her back was pretty bad, and she seemed to be tired the whole living time. 'I'm terrible tired,' she'd say in her croupy voice—'tired when I lay down, an' tired when I set up, an' nothin' don't seem to rest me any. Seems 's if I'd feel better if I could only walk round a mite, an' get out the dishes an' sasspans, an' grease the bakin'-plates, an' stone some raisins, an' chop some citron, an'— Oh, Aunt Eunice, I do want so bad jest to dish up a dinner once —only once, Aunt Eunice.'

"I didn't quite dare to do as Mrs. Peavy did, and tell her she'd have her chance some day, but I did go so far sometimes as to refer her over to Mother Peavy. 'What does she tell you, Colossy, when you talk so?' I said.

"Her face brightened up a little, and she answers, 'Oh, Mother Peavy says, when I get up there, if I'm set on messin' an' mixin' an' cookin' things, why, they'll let me try my hand at it. They'll know I 'ain't had no chance down in Peru, 'cause o' my hands an' my legs an' my back, you know, an' they'll make 'lowances. That's what they're allers a-doin' up there, Mother Peavy says, makin' 'lowances for folks. She says she don't think I'll want to do any dishin' an' bakin' up there, there's such splendid things to do that I don't know nothin' about now. She says nobody 'ain't never heerd nor seed, an' it 'ain't come into nobody's head to guess at sech things as they've got up there for folks that's good an' patient an' lovin'. But I don't

26

know; I'd like jest to try my hand a little, if they don't mind, seems 's if. An' if I do try, why, I'm goin' to see if they won't let me send down some o' my very fust cookin' to Mother Peavy. But if that can't be done, I mean to let her know, 't any rate, that she was right, an' they've let me try my hand.'

"She'd take some of the commonest, plainest kinds of food to experiment on, and she'd have a receipt for it with something in it you never dreamed of putting in before. Doughnuts, I know, she'd always say there was to be the third part of a hin of olive-oil in them. 'What's a hin?' I'd ask her; and she'd say, 'Well, about a coffee-cup full, I guess, more nor less.' And there was to be honey from the honey-comb in her dough-nuts, too. And in her apple-dumplings there 'd always got to be 'jest the teentiest pinch of aloes.' And all these victuals were to be fixed up in the tastiest way, and on the queerest kind of dishes. To hear the solemn little old-fashioned young one tell about 'butter in a lordly dish,' and meat cooked in a caldron or in a flesh-pot, or sodden in iron pans, and about brazen pots and earthen pitchers, was dreadful odd.

"She grew weak very fast near the end. She didn't go to bed, for it hurt her more to lie down, and they bolstered her up in her chair with the pillows, and made her as comfortable as they could. Her voice got more and more husky and low, down to a whisper, 'most, but she'd talk a little by spells up to the very last. She'd make up receipts still, but they were pretty short, and we couldn't always understand what she said. I stayed there all I could, and Mr. Robbins came a good deal, and old Mrs. Peavy hardly left her for days. She liked to hear verses about resting, and being carried, and made to lie down in green pastures, and having her tears wiped away, and about how the weary are at rest and the sick made well. But by spells she'd think about what she'd always set her little heart on, and she'd turn towards Mother Peavy and whisper, 'An' mebbe I'll be let to try makin' some of them things? 'Cause you know I've never had any chance down here, an' they'll make 'lowances for that.'

"And Mrs. Peavy 'd say, stroking her yellow

hair, 'Yes, lovey, they'll make 'lowances fast
enough. And you'll be let to do it certain
sure, if you hanker bad after it; don't worry
about that.' And then she'd say over to her,
in her thin old voice, her favorite piece about

> "'There cinnamon an' sugar grow,
> There nard an' balm abound,'

and another old-fashioned hymn, all about
milk and honey and wine and heavenly
manna, till Colossy 'd drop off to sleep like
a lamb.

"She went off that way at the last, bolstered up in the big chair by the window, her
poor white face resting against the pillows,
and her pretty yellow hair like a light all
round her head. David and Lucy Ann, Mr.
Robbins, Mother Peavy, and me were all
there. We loved her dearly, every one of
us, but somehow not one could be exactly
sorry when the tired look slipped off her
little thin face, and the bits of fingers stopped
twitching, and the hoarse, short breathing
was all still. I never thought as much of
Mr. Robbins as I did at that funeral. It
seemed as if he knew just the right things to

say that day—mostly verses from Scripture,
or a line or two of a hymn. I can hear him
now, speaking in his soft, pleasant way about
the 'bread that came down from heaven,'
'meat to eat that ye know not of,' 'whoso-
ever drinketh of the water that I shall give
him shall never thirst'; and those comforting
verses about how 'they shall hunger no more,
neither thirst any more,' and how 'blessed
are those that are called to the marriage-
supper.' And then he led off in his nice,
clear voice :

>　"'Food to which this world's a stranger,
>　　Here my hungry soul enjoys;
>　　Of excess there is no danger;
>　　Tho' it fills, it never cloys.'

"Well, 'twas about a week after we put the
little girl to rest in the graveyard over there
I met Mrs. Peavy one day. We stopped, and
naturally we fell to talking about Colossy.
Glad as I was to have the child at rest, I
missed her lots, and I said so.

"'You were real good to her, Mother
Peavy,' I said. 'I often think how you used
to comfort her, and tell her that maybe she'd

have a chance to try her receipts up there, if she wanted to. Dear little thing, she understands better now, and don't trouble her head about those earthly things.'

"Now, I'd always thought that Mrs. Peavy told the child that about having her chance up there just to chirk her up and please her, and not because she ever dreamt such a thing could really be. So I must say I was took aback when she shook her head now and answered in a queer, knowing sort of way, 'She 'ain't found out the better things yet, that's certain. She's got her chance, and she's a-makin' use of it right along; leastways, up to yesterday she was.'

"'Why, what do you mean?' I says. 'What makes you say that?'

"And then she went on and told me the oddest story. She said she'd been thinking and thinking about Colossy, and trying to picture her all well and rested and happy in heaven; but for the life of her she couldn't see her in her mind as singing and praising and doing all the things the saints and angels are said to do. The poor young one's talk about her wanting to dish up and mess kept coming into her head to spoil everything. One day she was sitting at her dinner. She lived all alone and did her own work. And that day she had what every one in these parts calls 'b'iled dish.' You know what I mean — beef and potatoes and carrots and turnips and all. And she says:

"'I'd jest helped myself, and was going to taste of it, when I smelt a queer kind of spicy smell. I couldn't think where it come from, or rec'lect jest what 'twas like. Then I took up a little of the meat and put it in my mouth, and I didn't know what to make of it. I'd made that b'iled dish that day with my own hands, just as I'd made it all my life, an' my mother before me. But this partic'ler one wasn't any more like mine or ma's or any Vermont b'iled dish I ever see than—anything. It was tastier, more flavory somehow, and, above, all there was that cur'us spicy kind o' physicky smell and taste. "What can it be?" thinks I to myself. "Is it cloves or saxifrax? Did I spill any nutmeg or ginger into the pot while 'twas b'ilin'? No, 'tain't like any of them. It's more like that rhubarb jellup I used to make after old

Dr. Phelps's receipt. Lemme see, what did I put in? Rhubarb root an'—why, it's coriander seed; that's what it tastes of!" And in a jiffy I rec'lected Colossy, and how she used to always say in her receipt for b'iled dish, "Add a little coriander seed brayed in a mortar."

"'Well, I didn't know what to think,' she went on. 'It seemed 'most too sing'lar to believe in. But to save my life I couldn't help surmisin' that maybe—jest maybe—they'd let her try, to show her how unsatisfyin' it was compared to other things up there. And she'd always said, if they did, she'd try to send some of the victuals down to me, the blessed young one!

"'I tried to get it out of my head and swallow my dinner; but, deary me, every mouthful choked me, and I salted the gravy with my cryin' into it, thinking of that poor little soul. Well, the next day was Saturday, and I fried some dough-nuts. The taste o' coriander seed bein' all out of my mouth now, I begun to think I'd conceited the whole thing and 'twas all foolishness. But when I set down to supper and took a dough-nut, I hadn't more'n bit into it than I see 'twasn't one o' my dough-nuts, Aunt Maria's receipt, sech as I'd made for more'n forty year. These was rich an' light, and sort o' iley, and there was a strong taste o' honey about 'em, a thing I never use in cookin'. Oh, Aunt Eunice, then I knowed, I knowed they was lettin' that poor child have her way for a spell, jest to learn her a lesson. "Fine olive-ile an' honey from the honey-comb," she used to say in her receipt for dough-nuts. And when the gingerbread tasted o' spikenard, and the apple-dumplings was jest a little bittery like aloes, and everything I made— or thought I made—was different from any Peavy cooking ever done in the family, then I see plain I was right. And it's only yes-terday I made—or thought I made—some one-two-three-four cake, the old plain receipt; and it came out the most cur'us, spicy, milk-an'-honeyish, balmy, minty thing—oh, you never did!'

"I tell you, as Mother Peavy went on I began to think she was really crazy. She'd always been a little peculiar, and she was growing old, and Colossy's death had weighed

on her mind, and I thought it had fairly upset her now. I tried to reason with her, and
show her how such a thing as she thought of
could never be. But I couldn't make any
impression. I told her it was dreadful to
think of heaven in that way, and that dear
little girl losing all the light and glory and
all, for such earthly, gross kind of employ-
ments. I couldn't bear to think of it. Mrs.
Peavy looked sort of mournful, and she says,
''Tis dreadful, I know. I did hope Colossy 'd
put it all out of her little head, once she got
there. But there can't be any mistake. If
I am old, I 'ain't lost my faculties, leastways
my taste, and I know what I've been eating
all this week. They've got some good reason
for it up there, take my word for that; but
oh, I do wish she'd learn about the better
things there is.'

"Well, I meant to go over and see the old
lady next day and taste some of her victuals
myself, to show her what a mistake she was
making. But I took a bad cold that night,
and didn't go outside the door for 'most a
week. The first day I was well enough I
started, but I met Mrs. Peavy coming over

to my house. It upset me to see her, she looked so terrible white and changed and old.

"'Oh, Aunt Eunice,' she says, 'it's dreadful, dreadful. That poor little thing's at it still. She's turning my sody biscuits into unleavened bread, and my pies into pottage; there's lentils in my corn-beef hash, and fitches in my johnny-cake; and oh, deary, deary me, there's mint, anise, and cummin in every bit of victuals that comes on the table. Poor ignorant little soul, what can she be thinking of! It jest breaks my heart, Aunt Eunice, for—oh, 'twas I done it, I done it!' and she just wrung her hands.

"It seemed she'd got it into her head that her tellin' Colossy she'd have a chance and they'd let her try things had made the poor child beg for it; and now she liked it so well, after never having had anything of the sort all her days, that she couldn't give it up. It seems a crazy idea, I know, but 'twas terrible real to her, and as she said herself, it 'most broke her heart.

"'I thought 'twould be sech a comfort,' she went on, 'to think of that child among the blessed ones, all straight and well and rested, all dressed in clean white robes, praising and worshipping and loving, walking along the banks of the river or down the streets o' gold. And now to think of her keepin' on and on this way—oh, 'tain't right, 'tain't right.'

"I saw she needed some one wiser and better than me, and I went that night to Mr. Robbins with the whole story. I'd calculated he'd be very much put out by such foolishness, and think it was wicked and making light of sacred things. But when I got through I saw his eyes looked kind of moist, and he had to cough and clear out his throat before he could say anything. So I spoke again to give him time, and I says, 'Mother Peavy's growing old and she's getting childish.'

"'Well,' says he, 'that's what we've all got to be to get at the truth of things. "Except ye become as little children," you know; and childish and unreasonable as the good old soul's idea is, there's a lesson in it. Let us go and see her.'

"And we did; but he couldn't do her much

good. She had got so upset and shaky that she couldn't do anything but cry and bewail her having put things into little Colossy's head and spoiled her heaven for her.

"At last Mr. Robbins said, 'Well, Mrs. Peavy, suppose we lay this before the Lord and ask His aid,' and then he prayed. I never shall forget that prayer. You see nobody but Catholics ever prayed for dead-and-gone folks then, and I suppose they don't now; and our church was always strong against it, of course. And I'd heard Mr. Robbins himself preach a powerful discourse about it from the text, 'Where the tree falleth, there it shall be.' But I suppose he saw now it was a time for strong measures, and, scruples or no scruples, he must quiet this good old soul. So he prayed for Colossy! I can't help thinking he meant that prayer more to help Mother Peavy than to do Colossy any good; but 'twas beautiful, 't any rate. Of course I can't remember just the very words. But he asked that the child might rest in peace and have light given unto her, that she might with the other little ones always behold the face of her Father.

And he asked that she might drink of the water of life, clear as crystal, and eat of the heavenly manna, and be satisfied. And he ended up by asking that her friends here below might be given the full assurance of the little one's peace and rest. In all the years he was settled in Peru I never heard him pray so earnest, and I was certain sure in my own heart he'd be heard. Then he asked Mrs. Peavy if he and I could come over next day and eat dinner with her. 'And you must have one of your good old-fashioned dinners for us, Mrs. Peavy,' he says, 'and we'll tell you just what we think of it.'

"So we went. She'd made b'iled dish, and it looked real tempting and just like her old way of making it, for she was a real good cook. But she was all shaky and trembly, her face looked drawn up and old, and she could hardly sit up to the table without help. Mr. Robbins asked a blessing, and then the dinner was helped. I'll own up I was a little nervous. The queerer the ideas, you know, the more catching they are. And I'd thought so much of what the old lady had said of the tastes and smells in her cooking lately that

39

I felt almost creepy with being afraid I should find it that way myself. 'Oh dear,' I says to myself, 'if there should be a coriander-seed flavor!' But there wasn't. Mr. Robbins began first, and I followed right away. It was the same good, well-seasoned, Peru b'iled dish I'd eat dozens of times before at that table. Mrs. Peavy didn't taste of hers at first. I really don't think she could raise her spoon to her mouth, she shook so. But she fixed her eyes on our faces, first one, then the other, leaning 'way over and looking and looking, as if she was hoping, but scared.

"'Well,' speaks up Mr. Robbins, 'this is good indeed. One of your best old-fashioned dishes, Mrs. Peavy. I should know that this was a Peru b'iled dish if I was a hundred miles away,' and he went on eating it.

"'Yes,' I says, following his example, 'I always liked Mrs. Peavy's way of making it —just the pepper-and-salt seasoning, and no flavors, as some folks use.'

"She looked real earnest at us, and then she says, low and quivery, 'Don't you—take notice—of a leetle—coriander-seed taste— just a leetle?'

"And we both hurried up to say there wasn't one bit of that—not a suspicion, Mr. Robbins said.

"She didn't look quite satisfied, though just a mite more comfortable. Then she took some of the gravy in a spoon with her shaking hand and put it to her mouth. She spilt some and she could hardly swallow any, but I see her face clear up a little, and she sort of whispered to herself, 'She's let that alone, anyway.'

"Then we had some apple-dumplings, and 'twas the same way. Mother Peavy waited and watched, half hoping, half frightened, till Mr. Robbins led off, eat some and praised them up, and I followed on.

"'An'—there—don't appear—to be—anything—a speck—bittery?' she says, leaning across to us and asking so solemn—'not enough to—spile 'em, but—something like—aloes?'

"And again we hurried on to tell her there wasn't a taste of such a thing, not a taste. Then she managed to swallow a little herself, and again I saw her features light up a mite, and she whispers to herself again, 'An' she 'ain't meddled with them.'

"After that came dough-nuts and cheese with our cup of tea, and that was just the same. After Mr. Robbins had praised them up, and I had done it after him, and she'd asked us in the same scared, nervy way if we was sure we couldn't taste a flavor o' olive-ile or honey, we told her decided there wasn't anything at all like that; they were just good, old-fashioned Peavy dough-nuts. They were the last thing on the table; she'd tried all the rest, and I saw she was more scared now than any time before, when she took one in her trembling fingers and tried to lift it up to her mouth. I thought for a minute I should have to do it for her, but she managed it somehow, and got a piece between her poor, shaking, twitching lips. I thought I was prepared for anything, worked up as I was over this. But I did break down like a baby when the good old soul burst out, the tears running down her wrinkled face in a shower, and the heavenliest smile shining through them like a rainbow, 'She's found it out—oh, bless the Lord, she's found it out at last! No more messin' an' fussin' with earthly things for Colossy Bragg. She's looked up higher, and seen the light at last. Oh, thank the Lord, thank the Lord!'

"We both went over to her. Seems to me now, as I look back, we was both crying, but I disremember all about that. We got her quiet after a spell, but for a long time she kept sobbing out, 'I'm so glad, I'm so glad. Your praying done it, Mr. Robbins. They've took the blessed child up higher now, and they've sent me word.'

"Well, there was a story went around the whole county, after that, that Mr. Robbins was on the road to Rome, as they said. Maybe you've heard it. It all came from that prayer he made at Mrs. Peavy's in behalf of little Colossy Bragg's soul. But, as I said before, it's my opinion that prayer was meant more to help the living than the dead, and somehow, some ways, it answered its purpose."

APPLE JONATHAN

APPLE JONATHAN

No one who knew the Stonington of thirty years ago can fail to remember old Jonathan Tripp, the apple-dealer. His quaint figure and wagon with its spicy load were as familiar to all who lived in or visited the village as was the Road Meeting-house, the old lighthouse on Windmill Point, or Roderick Nathan's store. But although I recall with wonderful distinctness the face, form, words, and actions of the old man, I find my memory failing me upon certain points of detail. I am not quite sure where his house and orchard were situated, but I have a strong impression that they were in North Stonington. I know that I often met him driving his wagon into the borough from that direction. Nor do I know if he himself raised all the fruit he sold, or whether he brought into

market the produce of his neighbors together
with his own. But I feel well assured that
never, before nor since, did I see or taste such
apples as those old Jonathan Tripp's wagon
bore.

He was not often called by his whole name.
The Stonington boy of that day had a rare
faculty for bestowing appropriate nicknames,
and to the old vender of the fruit so dear to
all New-Englanders they gave the name of
Apple Jonathan.

If you who read this sketch are of Con-
necticut origin, especially if you have ever
lived in dear, salty, rocky old Stonington,
you will not need that I should tell you of
the toothsome dish that bears this name.
Does not your mouth water, do not your
eyes grow moist, as you recall it, taken smok-
ing-hot from the brick oven, and sending out
the spicy, aromatic odors nothing else can
quite equal? Think of the golden-brown,
crisply tender paste, the rich flow of sweet
but piquant juice, redolent of cinnamon,
cloves, and I know not what else ; the delicate slices of apple cooked thoroughly, but
never too soft ; the—oh, you know it all. If

not, no words of mine can make you understand. And so old Jonathan Tripp was known
in the borough, in Milltown, Flanders, Mystic,
Pawcatuck, Voluntown, and for miles around,
as Apple Jonathan.

Day after day the black wagon, drawn by
the old gray mare, rattled along the road,
loaded with baskets and bags of the homely,
fragrant fruit. There were gillyflowers of
dark purple-red and pear-like shape; golden-
sweets big and yellow; the little Denison
reddings, all crimson and shining outside,
and with the white crisp meat streaked and
veined with red; Prentice russets of bronzy
brown, the larger and greener Cheeseb'rin'
russets, spicy red Spitzenbergs, Rhode Island
greenings, seek-no-furthers, scarlet Astra-
khans, pumpkin-sweets, Roxbury russets, the
Northern spy, the Newtown pippin, pear-
mains, red-streaks, sheep's-noses, Baldwins,
Peck's pleasants.

Then there were rare and choice varieties
with mysterious names, of whose origin Apple
Jonathan would never speak. Such was the
Lang'orthy fav'rite, a large, sweet, very juicy
fruit, its yellow skin thickly dotted with black.

Of this kind he was very choice, bringing but
a dozen or so at a time in a covered tin pail,
with a cloth tied down tightly over the lid.
Then there was the Tripp tart to bake for
invalids. These were so very rare as to be
brought by twos or threes in the pocket of
the old man's coat. I well remember the
smell and the taste of one of those brought
me when recovering from some childish ail-
ment. It was cooked in a delightful way,
suspended by a string from the wooden man-
tel, and revolving slowly in front of the hard-
coal fire in the grate of the keepin'-room.
A saucer was placed below, just inside the
fender, to catch and hold the dripping juice.
What matter if a little ashes fell down and
mingled with that syrupy stuff, half sweet,
half sour? I ate it all, that Tripp tart juice,
and longed for more. It was currently supposed that no perfectly sound and well person
had ever tasted a Tripp tart apple. Even
old Jonathan himself, when asked, once upon
a time, if he did not think this variety a little
sweeter than in old times, replied, doubtfully,
that he " wa'n't certain sure about it, for he'd
had a long spell o' good health." And I doubt

not that many a man and woman of to-day
finds the very name of Tripp tart a potent
charm, calling up a far-away childhood, a
restless night, an aching head, small burning
hands, or a shivery little body. Somehow
those childish pains and aches do not seem
so bitter in memory, and we think now a
good deal more of the cool soft hands which
touched the head and cheek so gently, turned
the hot pillow, and held the restless little
fingers.

Apple Jonathan himself was a tall, spare,
awkward man, with rounded, stooping shoulders, thin gray hair, and a lean, brown,
weather-beaten face. I can see him plainly
in recollection, with his shabby brown over-
coat, the gray-and-red woollen comforter tied
about his neck, the blue-yarn mittens, the
faded cloth cap drawn down over his ears, as
he drove day after day along the roads and
lanes. Now he would stop at Nabby Lord's
with some pie-apples for her Saturday baking, again at Uncle Sim Lewis's to leave
a bushel of the old man's favorite greenings, then down the lane by the old Trim-
ble place to take a Tripp tart to little

Billy Merritt, just getting up from scarlet-fever.

Again and again as he passed along he was hailed, sometimes by a woman with her shawl over her head, who would run out with a milk-pan for some golden-sweets for the children, or pippins for apple-sauce; sometimes by a boy or girl with a big copper cent to spend for juicy fruit. Again, it might be a man with an order for a barrel or two of gillyflowers or seek-no-furthers for the winter evenings. Large or small, the order was promptly filled, and the stock seemed inexhaustible.

But Apple Jonathan was not merely a dealer in apples; he was a lover of the fruit, which he knew thoroughly in all its forms, stages, developments. I do not mean simply that he understood its cultivation, preservation, and uses, though these he did understand well. But all his thoughts and his words were of his favorite fruit; he found in it something for every emergency; he used it for illustration, for suggestion, for moral lesson—everything.

"Tell me I set too much by apples," the

old man would say. "Why, I couldn't do it. There ain't no sech thing as settin' too much by 'em. They're the one thing in all this shaky, onsartin' airth of ourn that stands by you allus, an' don't never fail nor disapp'int. Set your heart on clothes, or houses, or live-stock, or even folks, and more'n likely they'll turn out as you don't want 'em to. Clothes will tear or rip or grow shiny most the fust time you put 'em on ; your new house will be draughty or smoky or leaky or suthin' ; your creatur's will ail, or fall into holes an' break their legs, or be struck by lightnin'; an' folks — well, everybody knows what folks is, an' how they ain't to be depended on for a stiddy supply o' comfort best o' times. But apples never disapp'ints ye. There they be, year arter year, seed-time an' harvest an' all, right by ye, never failin', never hurtin' ye, never turnin' out diff'ent from what you'd expected, an' ready for every single state o' mind or sitooation o' body you could git into. S'pose you've had a disapp'intment o' some kind, an' you've begun to feel as if there wa'n't any-thing to be depended on in this mortal airth, that everything's a fleetin' show for man's delusion given, that there ain't nothin' what it's made out to be, that 'each pleasure hath its p'ison too, an' every sweet its snare,' why, you jest go to your apple barrel for a gilly-flower, say, if that's the kind you like. You take a apple out, an' there 'tis. It's a gilly-flower, an' it's gillyflower color, dark an' pur-ply red like them hollyhawks by the fence there. It don't come out yeller like a golden-sweet, nor brownish like a Prentice russet, nor streaky like a Spitzenberg; it's just what it allus was as to color. Then it's gillyflower shape, too. 'Tain't big 'round an' squatty like a greenin', nor little like a Denison reddin'; but it's kinder long an' slopin', as gillyflowers allus was an' allus will be. Then you come to the proof o' the puddin', 's they say—the eatin'. You bite into it. 'Tain't so tasty an' high-flavored one way as a seek-no-further, nor so nice an' sweet as a sweetin', nor sech a pleasant tart as the Davis sour; mebbe 'tain't so good reely as any o' them kinds, but it's itself anyway, an' jest what you knowed 'twould be, mashy an' half an' half sorter, not very decided tastin' anyway, but it's gilly-flowery, an' that's what you want jest now, an' you says to yourself, 'Here's suthin' cert'-in, suthin' I can lot on an' never be disap-p'inted.' Tell me that don't help ye? It can't miss o' doin' it.

"Or s'pose ag'in you're sick, an' nothin' seems to do you any good—doctors' stuff, nor yarbs, nor nothing. Why, you have to come to apples. If you're run down an' pindlin', an' need stren'th'nin' an' stimerlatin', why there's new cider or old apple-jack to build ye up. Or ag'in, if it's t'other way, an' you're too hot-blooded an' filled up an' pulsy, why, there's nothin' so coolin' an' down-pullin' as a froze-an'-thawed apple on a empty stomach. If it's nettle-rash or erysipler, or any outside skin-ny thing like that, a poultice o' sour apples spread on is the best thing in the world—lots better 'n cramb'ry. For a hackin' cough you take apple surrup with a leetle bit o' flaxseed or slipp'ry ellum. For bitters, when you don't relish your victuals, why, you stick a Rhode Island greenin' full o' cloves, an' roast it 'fore the fire, an' when it's done through pour some New England rum over it—as much as it 'll soak up; sprinkle some dried tansy an' worm-wood leaves with a pinch or two o' camamile flowers over it, an' take it afore eatin'. There ain't nothin' apples can't cure, take it in time.

"But s'pose you ain't sick, but kinder tired o' meat an' potaters an' fish an' clams an' lobster, why, live on apples. There's apple-sass an apple-butter an' dried-apple pie an' green-apple pie, an' apple-dumplin's, an' apple turnovers, an' apple slump. There's steamed-apple puddin' an' bread - an' - apple puddin'. There's baked apples an' stewed apples an' preserved apples an' fried apples. There's apple jell an' apple marm'lade an'—why, you could live on nothin' but apples for a year, an' never have the same dish two days runnin' !"

And so the old man would run on as long as any one would listen to his talk. On topics of general interest he had nothing to say. He knew little of public affairs, politics, wars, or even the local village gossip. He was, according to most standards, a very ignorant man. He could read slowly and with difficulty, spelling out laboriously the larger words. He wrote a little, and knew enough of figures to "tot up" his accounts

in the apple trade. Not a very liberal edu-
cation, you see. But he had picked up much
odd, out-of-the-way information — religious,
biographical, historical — relating to his favorite theme. To humor his fancy, for he
was a general favorite in the town, people
brought to the old man any facts they could
gather relating to his hobby. And he laid
them away carefully, till his mind was a queer
storehouse, an apple - cellar, so to speak, of
pomological treasure. And he knew how to
bring out these bits of learning, casually as
it were, in his daily conversations, often giving one the impression that he was a student
and a thinker, and had read and absorbed
many books.

He did read his Bible a great deal. He was
a good, pious old soul, and if his religion
seemed strongly flavored by his favorite
fruit, can we blame or judge him? Is there
not decided individuality in each one's creed,
and do not our own peculiar tastes influence
strongly the hopes and fears of our theological sentiments? I never saw Apple Jonathan read any book but the Bible — an old
leather-bound copy which was his constant

companion — and a queer old hymn - book,
which he knew by heart. Of this last I know
but one copy, which is unique as far as I
know. Its title is *Divine Hymns, a Collection
by Joshua Smith and Others*, and it is full of
quaint verses, which the old man was fond
of repeating. I suppose that the principal,
perhaps the sole reason that it was included
in his small library was because of one hymn
which bore upon his beloved hobby. It is a
curious old piece, entitled "Christ, the Apple-
Tree." However strangely it may sound to
modern ears, it certainly did not strike any
of us who heard it in Apple Jonathan's thin,
quavering voice as irreverent, or lacking in
a sort of homely fervor. I quote here some
of the lines, and I can almost hear his very
tones, while a faint spicy odor, as from an
orchard, seems to fill the air :

" The Tree of Life my soul hath seen,
  Laden with fruit, and always green ;
  The trees of nature fruitless be
  Compared with Christ, the apple-tree."

One verse begins :

" I'll sit and eat this fruit divine;
It cheers my heart like spiritu'l wine ";

and this Jonathan would repeat with great feeling, thinking of his own beloved earthly fruit, though never forgetting, I am sure, the divine with its spiritual cheer.

There seems to be a good deal about fruit in that old book. Perhaps Joshua Smith and others had orchards too. One of them sings : •

" There we shall see that fruitful tree
Which bears twelve times a year,
Whose lovely fruits so sweetly suits
All heav'n's guests for cheer."

And another addresses

" My children dear that now appear
Like blossoms on the trees."

It is in this last hymn that the writer says:

" You know that then five out of ten
Of virgins did prove fools;
Why may not you be found so too,
If you take up their rules?"

Although this stanza bore no allusion to apples, Jonathan often quoted it. He was an old bachelor, and there was a tinge of something like contempt in the way in which he sometimes spoke of woman and her capacities. According to him, she judged an apple by its exterior, the color or gloss of its skin, or, worse yet, by its price, a very belittling thing to do.

"I never knowed a woman hardly," he would say, "that was a real jedge o' apples. They don't never seem to have what I call a tasty fac'lty. Course they can't help knowin' when a apple's out an' out sour, or up an' down sweet; but the betwixts an' betweens, the half-ways, the jest off one an' a mite on t'other, why, they can't ketch it— minds ain't strong enough. Why, there's Tildy Bliven, she makes a great time over my Lang'orthy fav'rites, an' one time I asked her what she held to be the p'int o' that apple, the thing that made it diff'rent from other apples; I jest wanted to see what she'd say; an' she says, 'Why, I call it sweet,' says she. 'Nothin' else?' says I. 'Why, it's awful dear,' she says; 'highest priced you've

got, 'most.' Now that shows. Why, any
man would 'a' told ye the main p'int of a
Lang'orthy fav'rite was juice, lots o' juice,
an' all on it with jest the leetlest taste an'
smell o' sweet - birch. I've knowed women
treat comp'ny—men comp'ny too, that knows
what good fruit is—to lady-apples, an' nothin' else, jest 'cause they was pink an' yeller,
an' looked pooty on a blue willow-ware plate!"

Apple Jonathan was an even - tempered,
kindly man, and rarely showed any acidity
or real bitterness in his feelings. The only
occasions on which I have seen him give
vent to much irritation or annoyance were
when any of the "city folks," summer visitors,
staying at the old Wadawannuck, made inquiries of him concerning some species of
apples unknown to him. That piqued and
vexed the old man sorely. I met him one
day, out on the east road, shaking his head
and muttering to himself, with a very troubled
look on his brown, wrinkled face.

"Jest come from the hotel," he said. "Man
from Philadelphy wanted to know if I'd got
any twenty-ounce apples. I wa'n't goin' to
let on I never heered on 'em, so I says:

' 'Tain't the season for twenty-ouncers. The kep'-over ones is gone, an' the new crop ain't ripe.'

" An' then a lady she run out an' she says : ' Ain't you got any New Jersey codlins? That's the only specie my husband can eat,' she says.

" Codlins ! codlins ! Better call 'em tom-cods an' done with it, an' buy 'em from Abel Wilcox, the fish-man. I 'ain't no patience with them 'ere furren fruits an' names. Every apple that's good for anything is raised in Stonin'ton borough, or within five miles on it, 't any rate."

We often teased the old man and tried to draw from him some of his odd information as to the fruit he sold, by pretending to decry it and seeming to doubt its close connection with the history of the universe.

" Why, what has it to do with geography, for instance ?" one of us would ask.

" Jography ? Why, it's got everything to do with jography. 'Tis jography itself. How does the books go to work when they want to lay down the very beginnin' o' things an' tell how the airth's shaped ? They say it's like a

apple, kind o' round, but a little flattened off
at the stem an' blossom ends. They couldn't
give no idea o' the airth if 'twa'n't for apples,
an' we might 'a' got to conceitin' 'twas narrer
an' p'inted like a pear, or skewy an' knobby
like a quince, or with a turnover handle like
a crook-neck squash, if we hadn't got jest the
thing to measure it off by."

" But history, Uncle Jonathan—how about
that ?"

" Hist'ry ? It's jest chock - full on 'em !
You rec'lect about the man that put the apple on his boy's head — a greenin', I guess
'twas ; that's flattest at the bottom, an' would
set good without jogglin'—an' fired at it. An'
then there's that story that's in all the school-
books, they say, about a prize apple they give
one time to the best-lookin' woman, an' the
time they had over it. It's jest so to-day
at our county fairs an' fruit shows ; there's
sure to be trouble about the premiums, partic'lar if there's women in it. But that
wa'n't in Conne'ticut, but out Troy way,
I believe. An' then there's that story they
tell about George Washin'ton an' his cut-
tin' his pa's apple - tree. Oh, hist'ry's jest

as full o' apples as this peck measure here is."

"But arithmetic — do apples come into that?" we would ask.

"More 'n anything else," Apple Jonathan would reply. "I hear the boys an' girls at Miss Lucy Ann's school sayin' their lessons when I'm waitin' outside, days. Teacher says, 'If John's got fifteen apples, an' he gives Mary six,' an' so on an' so on, 'how many,' she says, 'has he got left?' 'An' if a bushel o' apples cost so much,' says she, 'how much does a barrel come to?' An' so 'tis, over 'n over—apples, apples, apples.

"More 'n that, they can't learn young ones to read without 'em. I heerd Hepsy Pome‑ roy sayin' over her letters t'other day, an' 'twas all, 'A apple-pie, B bit it, C cried arter it, D danced for it,' an' so on an' so on, from A to Zed and Ampersand.

"What you gigglin' at now? They ain't got anything to do with courtin' an' love- makin'? Well, I don't know what's got any more. How'd you tell whether your sweetheart likes you or not 'thout namin' apples an' then countin' the seeds, an' sayin':

"'One I love, two I love, three I love I say,
Four I love 'ith all my heart,
And five I cast away,'

an' so on? Or ag'in, how'd you git the fust
letter of her name if you didn't have a apple-
parin' to throw 'round your head an' drop on
the floor? An' do you suppose there was ever
a couple kep' comp'ny here in the borough or
anywhere else 'thout a dish o' apples set out
when he come to see her? I was sayin' that
once to Elder Frink, o' West'ly, an' he laughed
kind o' foolish, an' owned right up that he begun courtin' Mis' Frink — she was Selmy
Noyes, ye know — by givin' her a bite of a
pumpkin - sweet at recess when he wa'n't
fourteen years old. You've got to ask me
suthin' harder 'n that.

"Now about the Scripters—that's the greatest. They're jest full o' apples. In the fust
place, in the very beginnin', ye know, there
was the gardin o' Eden, an' the best tree
there, the very ch'icest, everybody knows,
was a apple-tree. You rec'lect all that story,
an' you know what come on it. A apple was
the one thing Adam an' Eve couldn't stan'

bein' tempted by, an' they give way. So, you see, 'riginal sin, that the ministers make so much on nowadays, was started by apples. That wa'n't the fault o' the apples, but the folks that made a bad use on 'em.

"Then Solomon, he was the wisest man 't ever lived, an' he couldn't find a stronger comparin' or measurin' to use than to say, 'As a apple-tree is compared to other trees.' He set a great deal by apples, Solomon did. The Bible says he writ a book about trees, an' I often think I'd like to git hold on it an' see what he said about the Lang'orthy fav'rite, f'r instance. He talks about bein' 'under the apple-tree,' an' he says to his folks once, 'Comfort me with apples,' he says, showin' that he knowed what they could do to raise your sperrits an' chirk ye up when low in your mind. Why, the best thing he can liken a good, seas'nable, appropri'te sayin' to is to apples o' gold—golden-sweets, I s'pose—in picters o' silver, that is, set out on a shinin' pewter plate or Brittany waiter; 'tis as handsome 's a picter then, ye know.

"An' then Joel, one o' the old prophets, he tells about the apple-trees bein' all withered;

kind of a blight, ye see. To be sure, he mentions the palm-tree in the same c'nection, but that was a mistake, I guess. I dun'no' what palm-trees is good for except for fans to keep in the pews at meetin'.

"An' then there's one sayin' that's come down from them Bible times about the apple of our eye. That means the thing we've set our hearts on, the very best thing we've got —the apple, ye see, of our eye. They had to use the apple, ye see, to figur' that out too."

There was in the village at that time a boy named Joseph Peckham, but universally known as Joe Ricketts. His misshapen little figure, rounded shoulders, crooked legs, large head, and pale, thin face were well known to every one in Stonington. He was wonderfully intelligent, fond of reading, and had a remarkable memory. To this boy Apple Jonathan seemed greatly drawn, and the two were close friends. It was from Joe Ricketts that the old man learned much of the apple lore he dealt out with the fruit itself to his customers. It was little Joe who hunted out from books, papers, or magazines stories about the fruit, found out for his old friend the ori-

gin of the different names his apples bore, and
the history of each variety. I cannot remember them, those old tales. I do not know now
who was the Peck who gave his name to the
Peck's pleasant, nor the Denison who had for
namesake the little redding. I am not quite
clear as to which particular branch of the
Cheesebroughs belonged the discoverer of the
Cheeseb'rin' russet, nor why the Astrakhan
should bear that furry name. But Apple
Jonathan knew it all, and it was little Joe
Ricketts who told him.

There was one apple in the old man's orchard whose name puzzled both him and his
little humpbacked teacher. A young tree had
been given him years before by an old farmer
long ago dead, and to the best of Jonathan's
recollection he had called it the Neester apple-tree. That name was inexplicable to little
Joe. No such family as Neester was known in
the town, nor, as far as he knew, in the neigh-
boring villages. Neither was there any place
of that name known to the boy, or to any of
whom he made inquiries. He was piqued and
interested, and determined to solve the mystery. No trained antiquarian or philologist

could have thrown himself more eagerly into the question. He said the word over and over, suggested theories, and again demolished them.

"I wonder," said he, in one of his talks with Apple Jonathan, "if that tree didn't useter stand in the northeast corner o' the lot, an' so they came to call it the Nor'easter, an' then Neester?"

"That's so, sonny," said the old man; "that's reas'nable 'nough. Nor'easter; I bet that's how it come about. What a head you've got, Joe!"

"It's big 'nough, ain't it?" responded the boy. "But, arter all, I don't b'lieve it's Nor'-easter; it don't sound right somehow, does it?"

"No, it don't, it don't, sonny. Can't you hit on suthin' likelier?"

"You cert'in sure that farmer didn't call it the Yeasty apple?" asks the boy. "Then ye see it might be, 'cause it's kind o' light an' juicy like yeast emptins, ye know. Yeasty apple, wa'n't that it?"

"Mebbe 'twas, mebbe 'twas," the old man agrees. "But somehow I've allers rec'lected it as the Neester apple-tree."

"That's so," the boy would answer. "You wouldn't get it so dreffle diff'ent 's all that. No, it can't be Yeasty. But, deary me, what can it be, anyway?"

The farmer who had given this puzzling fruit to Jonathan was a Miner, and had lived at Quiambaug Cove, and to this place Apple Jonathan and Joe made several voyages of investigation. But they met with little success. Jubal Miner had died many years before, and none of his immediate family remained. He had never married, but lived with his brother's daughter Mercy, who, after the death of her uncle, had married and gone West.

"There!" exclaimed Joe Ricketts, one day, as he went over this part of the story; "I bet we've got it now. He lived with his niece, didn't he? Now, why didn't he name that apple arter her, an' call it Nieceter, 'cause o' her, his niece, ye know?"

"Jes so, jes so," says Apple Jonathan. "I rec'lect Massy Miner; she was a real likely gal; an' Jubal he sot everything by her. Neester, arter his niece; that's so, ain't it?"

"I d'no," says the boy; "it don't seem to

satisfy me some ways. If he'd wanted to name it arter her, he'd 'a' called it the Massy apple, or Massy's fav'rite, or suthin' like that. No, I ain't got it right yit."

After a talk of this nature one day, as the boy rode along the village streets by the old man's side, the wagon drew up before the green door of Miss Esther Carew. "Wait a minute, sonny," said Jonathan; "I promised to speak to Miss Easter about some pie-apples."

Now in Stonington, and through all New England, I think, the name Esther was pronounced Easter. It was often spelled so, and I have found it in that form on many an old gravestone. As Apple Jonathan came out of the back gate and rejoined the boy, little Joe cried out:

"I 'most b'lieve I got it this time. Wa'n't there an Easter 'mong Jubal Miner's folks, an' didn't he name it arter her, an' call it an Easter apple?"

"Sounds likely," responded Jonathan, "but I don't rec'lect any one o' that name in the family. We'll find out. I hope 'tis that way, for I allus liked that name. In my hymn-

book here there's a piece called 'Composed
on the Death of a Wife.' I've spoke it to
you, you know ; that one that says :

> " ' Now like a disconsolate dove
> I'm left all alone for to mourn.'

An' her name 'peared to be Easter, for in one
stanzy he says :

> " ' An' jine that eternal new song
> An' with my kind Easter to sing.' "

So to Quiambaug again they journeyed
to look for a possible Esther among Jubal
Miner's folks. But no trace of any one bearing that name could be found among the
Miners, nor in the closely connected families
of Wheelers or Yorks.

It was on a blustering day in early March,
as the old apple-dealer rode down the main
street of the village, that he saw Joe Ricketts
hobbling towards him up "the doctor's lane."
Joe waved his little thin hand, and Jonathan
stopped and took him in. The boy's face
was bright with excitement and interest.

"Mebbe — we've — got it this time," he
gasped, out of breath with his exertion.

"I jest came acrost it in a Sabba'-school book Ben Niles lent me. D'ye know there was another kind o' Easter?"

"No," said Apple Jonathan, in a surprised tone. "What is 't—a woman?"

"Oh no; it's a day—a day some folks keep. Jever hear of it, Uncle Jonathan?"

Now you must remember that the feasts and festivals of what is called the Christian Year were but little heeded at that time in Puritan New England. There was no Episcopal church then in Stonington, and in the other churches the custom of holding services upon Christmas or Easter was quite unknown. I doubt not there were many in the village and town who had never heard of Easter Sunday, though knowing well all about the glorious fact it is intended to commemorate.

So Apple Jonathan shook his head. "Never heerd of a day like that, Joe," he said. "What's it kep' for?"

Now poor Joe Ricketts was very close to being a heathen. There had been little in his wretched life to make him anything else. He remembered nothing of father or mother, but made his home—if we can give the place that beautiful name—with a crabbed, soured old aunt, who beat and abused the boy. Apple Jonathan, though a religious old soul, was reticent upon sacred themes, save so far as they seemed associated with his favorite pursuit, and had taught the boy little of what might have brought much light and comfort to the stunted, dwarfed soul shut up in its queer, battered cage. I will not give you the story of Easter as the boy told it. You would hardly recognize the tale in its quaint, homely form. But Jonathan knew it for what it was. His wrinkled brown face took on a softened look as he interpreted the story, and with the aid of his old Bible and hymn-book tried to make it clear to little Joe. This is no place in which to say much of that, nor of the hope which began to dawn in the boy's soul of a possible change some day in the rickety, aching body he dragged about so wearily. But after all, though there was such an Easter as this, what had Jubal Miner's apple-tree to do with it ? Neither Jonathan nor Joe could explain this.

"Did the book say what time o' year this Easter come ?" asked Jonathan.

"Said it changed about a good deal, but 'most allus come along in April somewher's."

"April! There ain't no apple-tree bears that time o' year," said the old man.

"Mebbe this kind keeps over till April better 'n t'others," suggested Joe.

"No," said Jonathan; "they don't keep good anyway. Fac' is, they ain't good for much, them Neester apples, 'tany rate late years. The leaves was all eat up this year an' last by caterpillars, an' the fruit wasn't much but windfalls, an' I left 'em on the ground; didn't pay to gether 'em."

Many and long were the conversations held upon this theme by the odd pair of friends. Their world was very small, and this question of the Neester apple's origin, so trivial to us, assumed vast proportions. Little Joe found much about Easter in his books, now that he looked for it, and he asked many questions of the minister and others well informed on the subject. But nothing helped him to make out the connection between the anniversary and the gnarled, worm-infested apple-tree. At last he read in the New London weekly paper that Easter would that year fall upon the 20th of April, and the boy looked forward eagerly to the day. Somehow he would know all about it then, he thought; something would happen. "I hope 'twill be nice weather," he said, "so 't I can set out an' watch, an' I b'lieve I'll find out the reason o' that name."

Apple Jonathan was to take the boy home with him on Saturday, the 19th, and keep him over Sunday. It was an early spring for that climate, and there had been a succession of soft, warm days, with the sun almost hot at noontime, though the nights were still cold. It was warm that Saturday morning as Apple Jonathan and Joe Ricketts started on their drive out to the old man's home. Joe thought it was too warm, took off his ragged woollen comforter, and said his hands and cheeks were "burnin' up." And surely there was a crimson spot on each thin cheek, and the little fingers felt very hot when Jonathan touched them. The boy was strangely excited, for they two were going to keep Easter, their first, under the Neester tree. April is an uncertain

month, particularly so in New England, and
before they reached Jonathan's house the
sky had clouded and a cold wind had come
up. And when the old man lifted the boy
down he was blue and shivering.

It was from old Jonathan himself that I
heard the story of that Easter. The morning dawned sunshiny and fair, and the pair
of friends were early at their post. There
was nothing of awakening or reviving about
the Neester apple-tree. Some of the early
fruit already showed small pink buds, and
there were leaves of tender green on many
trees. But Jubal Miner's tree looked brown
and dead. They sat down under it, and
again little Joe questioned Apple Jonathan.
He asked him about the blowth, the fruit,
the leaves, and finally about the caterpillars
that devoured the foliage. "Oh, they was
jest these pesky little things," the old man
told him, "that spin down on ye by a thread,
ye know ; the kind that go along, fust their
heads an' then drorin' up their tails, hunch-
in' their backs up every time, ye know."

"Like me," said the boy ; "I've seed that
sort ; allus makes me feel 's if they was mock-

in' me an' my way o' gettin' along. An'
what become on 'em, Uncle Jonny?"

"What, the wu'ms, sonny? Why, I killed
all I could on 'em ; an' the rest—there, now,
they was suthin' cur'us about that ! I forgot
it till now. I see some on 'em let theirselves
down off the tree, an' then what d'ye think
come on 'em ? Why, they dug down inter the
groun' like a mole, an' there they stayed."

The boy raised himself on his elbow and
looked into the old man's face. "Buried
theirselves in the groun'," he said, "an' stayed
there !" He shivered. "Wish ye hadn't tole
me that," he said ; "that's what I'm scared
of."

"What, of bein' buried, sonny? You hadn't
oughter talk that way ; 'tain't good for little
boys."

"Yes," in a low, frightened voice. "Aunt
Viny says I ain't never goin' to grow up ; an'
if I don't, why, that means I'm goin' to be put
in the groun', like Jim Fannin', an' it scares
me so !"

"But, bubby, you mustn't think o' that part.
Don't ye rec'lect what I told ye about the
risin' an' all that ?"

"I know," sighs the boy; "but I can't make it out real, someways. It don't seem reas'na-ble, does it, now, that you put me down in the dirt there, a drawed-up, hunched-up chap like them caterpillars you tell on, an' spect me to come out ag'in, an' all diff'ent an' spry an' flyin';—it don't, does it, now, Uncle Jonny? Might jest 's well think as how them hunchy wu'ms that went down an' died undergroun' there was goin' to come back ag'in." As he spoke, the boy, still leaning on one elbow, sift-ed through the fingers of his other hand the earth, lifting and letting it fall idly. In doing this he uncovered something small and hard and brown. "There, that's one on 'em now!" he said, in a weary tone; "all dried up an' dead 's a nail, jest 's I'll be, arter a spell." He touched it with his finger. Suddenly his face flushed and his eyes grew bright. "Uncle Jonny, quick! look! Suthin's happin' to it! Look! look!" Together the two bent over the dry, horny thing. And something did happen. It was an every-day, common thing, not a miracle. We do not believe in miracles in these days when we know so much. But it was a strange and wonderful thing to those simple folk. The bursting shell, the waking life, the spreading wings, the flight—oh, it was a glorious Easter lesson !

And when I saw, only a few days later, the rough, strangely shaped coffin that held the quiet form of poor Joe Ricketts, I thought less of the little grave just dug in the moist earth of the grave-yard than of the waking at another Easter.

"There 'tis, ye see," said Apple Jonathan, setting down his wooden peck measure while he wiped his eyes with his big red handkerchief ; "even that has to be learnt ye by apples. Sin an' dyin' come in by 'em, ye know, an' it looks now 's if they went out same way. Never made that little feller take in the doctrine o' risin' from the dead till we come to the apple-tree for 't. I'm dreffle glad he got a leetle comfort out on it ; though anyway he'd 'a' found it all out pooty soon, where he's gone. But I kinder miss him, an' even apples don't seem to help me 's much 's you'd think."

What mattered it that I learned long after from Elder Browning the true origin of the name old Jubal Miner had given his seedling apple, and that he had called it after his dead sweetheart, Esther Swan, for whose sake he had lived solitary all his days? The lesson was the same, and so was the comfort it brought to one poor little crawling, hunchy, human earthworm.

ANNA MALANN

ANNA MALANN

A GROUP of boys ranging in age from six to twelve, a small dog in the midst held tightly, while five little heads, brown, black, flaxen, and fiery red, all bent closely over the animal; a river conveniently near — what wonder that I thought I understood the scene! I had looked upon so many such, the surroundings, the actors, the little victim, almost identical. I love dogs, I am very fond of boys, but somehow I do not always enjoy seeing the two classes together. It was a hot still day in August. We were driving down from the mountains towards our home in southern New England, not by the direct and shortest route, but by a wandering, circuitous way, changing our plans from day to day, to suit our own or our horses' tastes or convenience. A rambling, lazy, hot - weather sort of journey it was. We had spent the last night at Morris, and were now going to Thacherville, some fifteen miles away. Our road was a pleasant one, along the bank of Wild River. St. - John's-wort, wild sunflowers, black-eyed-susans, the earliest goldenrod, and all the yellow and orange blossoms with which August shines and flames, grew along our way. Sometimes the vivid red of the cardinal-flower flashed upon our sight, and asters of every tint, from white to deepest blue and purple, starred the roadside. I was very comfortable, lying idly back in the carriage, and looking out at the birds and flowers and butterflies, and did not care to move. But the little group attracted my notice, and I called a halt. Stepping from the carriage, I walked towards the boys, ready with the appeal I had so often made in behalf of my dumb favorites. They were so absorbed that at first they took no notice of my approach. But in brushing through some tall plants a cracking twig or stem roused them, and one or two, turning, held up warning fingers or shook their heads to express disapproval of my coming nearer. Fired with missionary zeal, I kept on my course and walked quickly towards them. Suddenly one of the group, a brown-faced, barefooted little chap, some ten years old, started on tiptoe to meet me. He did not speak till quite close, and then it was in a whisper. "Please don't come any nigher, lady," he said; "you'll frighten him."

"What do you mean?" I cried. "What are you doing to that dog? Tell me this instant."

"Oh, don't, don't speak so loud!" he said, still in that same whisper, while again from others of the group came those silent signals of warning and disapproval; "he's dreadful bad, an'"—with a quaver in the low voice— "we think he's a-dyin'."

There was no mistaking the look in the boy's misty eyes and the tremble in the tones. I lowered my voice in sympathetic comprehension, and only saying, "Let me come; I won't disturb him," I stepped softly towards the little company. I had thought I might be of use, knowing a good deal of animals and their ailments, but at a glance I saw it was too late. The fast-glazing eyes, though still looking up with a pathetic attempt to express appreciation of the fond care shown him by his young friends, the convulsive twitching of the little form, showed he was, as my guide had said, "a-dyin'." So I was still and silent, for I was not needed. Doggie lacked nothing; love, sympathy, sorrow, tender care, they were his in abundance.

He was not a pretty dog nor of high lineage. He was a mongrel, of yellow and white, a thin, bony, ugly little fellow. But no dog of song or story ever had truer friends. He lay across the knees of one of the boys, while the others knelt or crouched or stood around, and all watched silently and sadly the passing of the—soul? Or shall we call it instinct? It was life, at any rate, and it was fast going out. It was soon over, and very quietly. The faintest movement of the poor stump of a tail—a pitiful attempt at a wag, poor beastie —as the youngest mourner, a mite of a fellow, touched with tiny brown fingers the rough coat of the sufferer, and all was ended.

As I looked about upon the sorry little

faces, the wet eyes, the quivering lips, I felt I must be dreaming. Was this a real dog, and were these boys? The little fellow whose knees had made the dying-bed for the animal did not at once rise or move, though he must have been stiff and aching from the constrained position in which for an hour he had been obliged to sit. As we lifted the limp little form from his lap, I asked him if the dog was his own.

"Oh no, ma'am," he replied; "he's a stranger to all of us. Johnny—that's my brother there—found him layin' in the road back a little way. I guess he'd been run over, an' he was real bad. So we fetched him here, an' was goin' to carry him down to the Gore, but we see he was a-dyin' fast, and we didn't take him."

"To the Gore?" I said. "What's that?"

The boy looked puzzled. "Why, the Gore," he said again. "We allers take 'em there, you know."

"I'm a stranger here," I explained, "and do not understand. Is it the name of a place?"

"Oh yes, 'm, I thought you knowed. Wilson's Gore, they call it, 'bout half a mile from here, out that way. There's jest nine families live in it, that's all. We're all Gore boys, us here; our folks live there; an' so o' course we knowed where to fetch the poor dog."

Then turning to the rest, he added, "But she can't do him no good now. Anyway, I s'pose we'd better take him over to her an' see what she says 'bout buryin' him." All signified approval, and I was more than ever puzzled.

"Does the dog belong to some one at the Gore?" I asked, but was again met with the assurance that he was a stranger, and nothing was known of his home or folks. "But why do you take him to the Gore, then?" said I.

"Why, to Anna Malann, o' course," he answered.

"Yes," said another little chap, "we allers fetch 'em to Anna Malann, even when they're dead."

By this time my friends in the carriage were growing weary of the long delay, and I was obliged to rejoin them hastily.

But I was determined to know more of

this mysterious Gore, and of Anna Malann herself. At the inn a little farther on we made inquiries and obtained some information on the subject. Wilson's Gore was one of those bits of land, occasionally found even now in New England, which were left between the boundary-lines of different land grants, and sometimes failed to be included in townships.

In this little spot lived nine families, as I had been told by the boys. And through the example or influence of one Anna Malann, an old woman in the place, every one there seemed to treat dumb creatures with strange consideration. About this matter the landlord said little, but advised me to go and see for myself. "She'll like to see ye," he said, "partic'lar if you like creatur's. An' it's dreadful amusin' to hear her talk."

Of course I went. I do like "creatur's," and my curiosity and interest were strangely excited by what I had seen and heard concerning Anna Malann and her missionary work.

I had not far to go. The inn itself was in Thacherville, but the boundary-line between

that village and Wilson's Gore was but half
a mile beyond. And the Gore once reached,
the house I sought was easily recognized
from the description of my landlord: "A little house that looks as if folks was movin' or
cleanin' house, and sounds like a menagerie."

I knew it at once by sight and hearing
both—a small house surrounded apparently
by rubbish — boxes, barrels, tin cans, crates,
baskets, scattered about in confusion. And
out upon the warm, soft air floated strange
sounds — whines, mews, barks, whinnies,
chirps, squeaks, cluckings, chatterings. Yes,
this surely was the abode of my home missionary. The door was open, and just within
it stood a thin, pale little woman stirring
with an iron spoon some mixture in a tin
pan. As I approached she looked up, and I
saw that she had soft brown eyes, with a certain wistful, gentle look often seen in the
eyes of an animal, especially an intelligent,
affectionate dog. You may think this fanci-
ful ; perhaps it is. Perhaps I was uncon-
sciously influenced to make this comparison
by what I had heard of the woman's tastes
and characteristics. But this I know, that

since I first saw her I can never look into the true eyes of my brave dog Larry without a quick memory of Anna Malann and her gentle face.

" Miss Malann ?" I said, inquiringly, as her eyes met mine and then turned quickly and shyly away, making them more than ever like Larry's, so averse to meeting a prolonged human gaze.

" No, ma'am ; my name's Ellis—Ann Ellis. Won't you walk in ?"

" Why," I said, somewhat puzzled, " I thought Miss Malann lived here. Miss Anna Malann the boys called her."

She interrupted me with a smile. "Oh, the boys ! Well, I guess they said Animal Ann ; that's what they call me, 'cause of my setting more 'n most folks by creatur's Don't wonder you didn't get it straight, not knowing about my queer ways and all. But come in, come in."

Animal Ann ! Why, of course it was plain enough now when explained, and I looked with fresh wonder and reverence upon one whose very bearing of the title seemed to give her a sort of canonization.

I want to tell you as simply and truly as possible the story of this woman. I shall try to quote her own words in what she herself told me, and to describe without exaggeration or sentimentality what I saw of her life and work. I use the word "story," but in one way there is to be no story. This is a mere descriptive sketch. There is no plot, little incident, and no *dénouement*. For, thank God! the life is still being lived and the quiet, unobtrusive work going on in, and farther and farther beyond, the tiny hamlet of Wilson's Gore.

I hardly know where or how to begin. But perhaps I had best tell first one little incident which seems to mark the key-note of the whole tale.

As we were walking out that first day among the boxes, barrels, and baskets which proved to be the humble dwelling-places of Animal Ann's favorites, I said:

"Why, how many animals have you here?"

She turned quickly towards me, her finger uplifted with a "Hush-h-h!" of warning. As I stared in perplexity she whispered in my ear, " They don't know they're animals; they think they're just folks."

And that gives one a pretty good notion of her ideas and her mode of treatment. I shall let her speak for herself now. She told me the story then, and I wrote it down directly afterwards, while the words were fresh in my mind. And many times since then I have heard her tell it to others. For the friendship begun that day has lasted and grown, and again and again, as the summer comes, I find my way to Wilson's Gore and the little home of Animal Ann.

" I don't know exactly how it come about, my taking to dumb creatur's, as they call them—though I must say I never see one that was anyways dumb myself. I lived over to Danvers, in the east part of the State, you know. Pa was a real good man, kind to his folks, a church-member, and one of the select-men of the borough. He was brought up in the strict up-and-down old-fashioned way as to religion, and had some pretty hard notions about some things. He had a good deal of stock—horses and cows and oxen and so on—and he took good care

of them, gave them plenty of food and drink
and good sleeping-quarters, and never beat
them, or let his hired men do it. But he had
views about animals that he'd picked up
from his father before him, and from old
Mr. Luther, his minister. I supposed they
was all right, 'cause pa held them, but even
when I was a mite of a girl they struck me
as queer and sort of ha'sh. He was good to
his stock, as I said before, but he insisted
that was only just because they was useful to
him and he wanted to keep them that way.
He was kind to Leo, the collie-dog, but he
said that was because he was so handy about
driving the cows and finding the sheep, and
he couldn't spare him. He was dreadful
good to the cats, but, according to him, that
was because of their catching the rats and
mice. But he was pleasant to the squirrels
too, and the robins, and the brown thrashers
—fed them and all—and he couldn't give no
other reason for that than this — that he
wanted to. ' But,' says he, ' animals haven't
got no rights ; that's a well-known fact. The
Bible don't give them any ; the Church don't
give them any ; the catechism don't give

them any. If I'm made so soft like and nervous myself that I can't see a creatur' hurt or
abused without its making me uncomfortable
and fidgety, why, that's my lookout. It don't
go to show I'd ought to feel that way. I
tell ye, if folks go to preaching that kind of
doctrine, that creatur's have rights, and I'm
bound to treat them as well as I do folks,
why, I'll just turn about and abuse them,
spite of my creepy, nervous feeling about
it. Same rights as folks? Why didn't God
make them folks, then?'

"So he'd go on and over with such talk,
and I'd listen and bother my poor little head
trying to make it sound right and reasonable.
'Why ain't they folks, anyway?' I says to
myself. 'What makes the difference? They
act like folks : they're good or they're bad ;
they're lazy or industrious ; they're noisy or
quiet, pleasant or ugly, selfish or free-handed,
peaceable or snarly. In short, they've got
ways. There's no two creatur's just alike, no
more than there is folks. They take sick like
folks, too, and they don't like to suffer no
more'n folks do ; and, come to the last, they
die like folks. And why does pa put them

all together, and say none of them haven't got any rights?'

"Sometimes I'd ask ma—I didn't quite dast to ask pa ; children didn't use to talk so free to their fathers as they do these times—I'd ask ma why animals wasn't folks, anyway. And she'd tell me 'twas 'cause of their not having souls — immortal souls. At first I used to go on and ask how folks knew creatur's hadn't got immortal souls, but she shut me up directly about that, and showed me right off that that was given up to by everybody—'twas one of the doctrines, and wasn't to be argued over ; 'twas settled for good an' all. So I never brought up that part again. But I'd bother and pester ma to know why, anyway—even agreeing 'twas that way—they wasn't folks just the same, and all the more to be pitied and done good to and made much of because they didn't have everything we had—souls and all them things. So whenever I got the chance I'd treat them that way, and try to make other people do it. But I couldn't make much headway. I had two brothers and one sister, and they all followed pa and ma's lead, and didn't worry them-

selves about the 'lower beings,' as pa called
them. Bime-by pa died, and a spell afterwards ma went too. And we four children
had the farm and stock and all to divide even.
Well, maybe 'twas foolish, but I'd been thinking and bothering my head so long about animals and the awful things that was always
being done to them, I couldn't get on any
other track. I suppose I took after pa in
being soft and nervous about such things,
and seemed to me there wasn't a minute of
the whole living day that there wasn't something cruel and unjust and dreadful done to
poor helpless creatur's even right around
me ; and what must it be, take the whole
world over ? I says. I was nigh about crazy,
and I'd seem to hear such a noise of whips
swishing and sticks pounding and kicks
sounding hollow against creatur's' sides, and
then a whining and moaning and whimper-
ing and crying out of the beings folks calls
dumb, and my ears ached and buzzed all the
blessed time. I couldn't stand it anyhow. I
was always a meddler and fusser, different
from the rest of the family, and I made up
my mind I'd got to have a finger in this

pie. I talked to Mary, my sister, and to Elam
and John, and tried to explain my views. I
wanted—well, I don't believe I had any real
settled plan laid out, and I don't wonder
now they thought I'd gone clean out of my
wits. But I tried to get them to let me try
what I could do on the farm and in Danvers
generally to make creatur's more comfortable
and get people not to put upon them so. But,
my! they got dreadful worked up over it.
You see, the Ellises had always been a respectable, quiet, contented kind of family,
holding the same ideas from generation to
generation, with nothing upsetting in their
religion or politics or schooling. They'd all
thought alike for a hundred years or more,
and they boasted there'd never been a schis-
matic or a heretic or a turncoat of any sort
in the whole tribe. And now to see an Ellis,
and a female one, too, set up for a stirrer-up
and overthrower, a sort of a horse-doctor and
dog-missionary mixed up, why, they wouldn't
have it. We had words, and, to make a long
story short, we settled it this way: I was a
sort of a mean-spirited, easy-going, anything-
for-peace woman myself, and so I just told

them I'd give up every bit of my share of the old farm to them three for nothing, and go off somewhere to try my plan. And they agreed to that, and let me go.

"Then I begun to look about to find the right kind of place. I wanted to see if there was such a thing as bringing over a whole community to my way of thinking. If I could be the means of getting everybody in just one town or village to try treating animals as if they was folks, why—well, 'twas something to live for, anyway. I considered and considered, and bime-by this notion came to me: I must find a small enough place so 's I could work it all up before I died; the Ellises ain't a long-lived family, and I wanted dreadful bad to see the whole thing done in my lifetime. 'Why,' I says to myself, 'it would be almost like a little millennium of my own.' Then I heard one day about Wilson's Gore, and it appeared to me just what I wanted. Six families in all—that's what there was then—and not very big ones neither. I had a little money besides my share of the farm I'd give up—some left me by the Aunt Ann I was named after, so I'd got something

to start with. And here I come, and here
I be.

"It's a good many years now, for 'twas
dreadful slow work. But it's done. Every
single one of the Gore families—and, as I said
before, there's nine now—has come over to
my way of thinking, and yet I ain't reached
the average Ellis limit of age yet. So I've
got my little millennium, you see. But I
must tell the whole truth and own up to one
thing. I don't believe I've had much to do
with it, after all. Come to think of it, I believe the Gore folks would have come to the
same p'int if I hadn't been here at all. For
I've never preached about it or scolded and
fretted at them or anything. They must
have had a leaning that way themselves, and
found it all out without my help. Sometimes
I wish I'd 'a' taken a harder place, with crueler
folks in it; there'd have been more credit in
that. For I've had an easy, comfortable time
of it, after all, doing for the dogs and horses
and cats that was sick or hurt or old or lost
or left out some way. You see, I like them,
and so it's dreadful interesting. And I like
showing them to folks, too, particular the

boys and girls. And they'll spend hours at a time watching me take care of them and talk to them and treat them my way. But as for preaching at them about it, or to their fathers and mothers, I hadn't got time for it. But there ain't a man or woman or a boy or girl now in the Gore that would do a cruel thing to a horse or a dog or a cow or an ox or any four-footed thing ; and, what's more, they wouldn't stone a bird or break up a nest —and children do like that kind of thing, you know ; and there even appears to be a feeling among the babies themselves against pulling off flies' wings and squeezing them to hear them buzz, and little amusements like that. They're terrible good children by nat- ur', you see, and I'm afraid I'll have to move. There ain't no satisfyin' field for real mis- sionary work here."

Before this little autobiography was ended we were walking out among the "creatur's," and I had many an object-lesson to illustrate Ann Ellis's mode of treating her friends.

Such odd friends they were, but I would not wish for truer, more loyal ones. Dumb ! Why, every soft wistful eye, each pricked-up

silky ear, each tail that wagged or thumped
the ground at the sound of her gentle foot-
fall, each pawing eager hoof and quivering
dilated nostril, spoke clearly, sharply, out of
love and trust and willingness to serve. Here
in the little pasture-lot grazed a blind horse;
there, a little away, an old and grizzled one,
passing his last days—his happiest ones, poor
fellow!—in peace and comfort. There were
dogs with bandaged, splintered legs, dogs that
were hurt or ill, lying on soft beds in basket,
box, or barrel. And there were well, active
animals, dogs and cats, and others too. Some
were waiting to be claimed by owners from
whom they had strayed away. Others had
been wilfully deserted, and had no home but
this. There was a lame hen hobbling about
on an awkward wooden leg; there was a
blind canary in a rough home-made cage,
singing his little heart out as he heard the
voice of the one he had never seen, but loved.

It was, as the landlord had said, "dreadful
amusin'" to hear Animal Ann talk, but it was
more. There was to me something strangely
pathetic, touching, in the way she spoke of
and to these creatures. Certainly there was

in her words or tones or looks nothing that could hint to these friends of hers that she thought them anything but "folks."

"Do you know how to talk French?" she asked, suddenly, one day. As I owned to some knowledge of the language, she said: "Oh, I'm real glad. You see, the children come over one day last month to tell me that the old monsheer, as they called him round here—him that used to learn the young folks to dance over in Danvers—was dead, and he'd left a dog unprovided for. The town had buried the old man, and the poor little creatur' was crying herself to death over the grave. I went over with them, and we fetched her away, dreadful unwilling, but too weak from mourning and going without victuals and sleep to make much fuss. I've brought lots of sorrowing young things through their troubles, homesickness and lonesomeness and disappointment and grief, but I never had a worse case than this. 'Twas a poodle; Fan Shong the old man used to call her; sounds kind of Chinee, don't it, now? And she was the miserablest being! She wouldn't make friends, she was scary and terrible bashful,

and she just about cried her eyes out after
that old master of hers—an outlandish, snuff-
taking, fretful little man to most folks, but the
best and dearest in the world to Fan Shong.
I tried hard to help her, to make her feel at
home, and show her there was something to
live for still, but she didn't take any notice.
I'd make a good deal of her, praise her up,
and call her ' good dog, good dog,' but she
didn't appear to care. And then bime-by it
struck me she didn't understand ; she was
French, and ' good dog' was no more than
foreign talk to her. Of course I had to do
something about it or she'd 'a' died on my
hands. I inquired about, and found there
was a lady over in East Thacherville, about
four miles from here, that knew some French
—used to learn it to children in the academy.
So I went over there. 'Twas a real hot day
in July, and there'd been quite a spell of dry
weather, and 'twas terrible dusty. I'd been
up all the night before with Charley, the old
white horse there, and didn't feel very rugged
that day, and I thought I'd never get there.
But I found Miss Edwards, and she was real
good, took quite an interest, and she learnt

me to say 'good dog' in French—'bong shang,' you know. I practised it over and over till I said it real good, and then I started home. Well, will you believe, time I got there it had gone clean out of my head. You see, I'd got it mixed up with the poor dog's Chinee name, Fan Shong, and for the life of me I couldn't say it right. So back I had to go through that dust and all and learn it again. But my! it paid, for she was so pleased when I told her she was a 'bong shang,' just as her old master done it. She's bashful yet, though, and lonesome, and she'd admire to hear her native language."

You may be sure I aired my best Parisian French for the benefit of the homesick for-eigner, greatly to the delight of my good old friend. Noting how careful she was lest any word of ours should hurt the feelings of her protégés, I asked her if she thought they un-derstood what was said.

"Well, I don't really know," she answered; "and so I go on the plan of acting as if they did. It don't do any harm, you see; and just supposing they do know our language, why, they'd be dreadful cut up sometimes. So I act as I do with folks, and mind my words when they're around."

It was a good while before I became used to this peculiarity of the old woman, and I was puzzled and startled again and again by a warning word, look, or gesture when about to speak freely of those about us. "That looks like a good hunting-dog," I said one day, pointing out a fine Irish setter near by. A significant look from Ann, a loudly spoken "Ain't he a nice dog? Yes, Jack's a good dog"—which words set the silky tail of golden-brown waving like a banner—and then the old woman whispered in my ear: "He's gun-shy, poor fellow. He can't help it; it's born in him. He's tried and tried, but he says he can't stand it. Just the very sight of a gun of any sort, loaded or not, scares him to death. That's how I got him. Jim Merrill had him, and was bound to train that trick out of him. He beat him till he 'most killed him, but it only made him worse. And so I bought him."

I shall never forget the confusion and shame which overwhelmed me one day at a reproof—a pretty sharp one—from the good old philanthropist. Peering out at us from behind a shed was the oddest creature. It was intended, doubtless, for a cat, but was such a caricature of one. One ear stood sharply erect, the other lopped limply down ; the eyes, because of an injury done to one of them, had a chronic squint ; and there was a twist upward to each corner of the wide mouth that suggested the grin of the pro-verbial cat of Cheshire. It was irresistible, and I—laughed. Animal Ann clutched my arm. " Stop laughing," she whispered, sharp-ly ; "or if you can't hold it in, go away." I was sobered at once. " Poor Jinny," said the old woman, after we had left the spot, "she's terrible homely, and she knows it as well as we do. Nobody'll have her, she looks so bad. And the worst of it is she's just aching to be made much of and coddled. There's the lov-ingest heart in that poor outlandish-looking body. She's real touchy about her looks, particular her eyes—maybe you took notice there's a mite of a cast in them—and I do all I can to make her forget about it."

The good woman even attributed to these animals theological creeds of their own, or rather, perhaps, adherence to those of the particular sect to which their former masters or owners belonged. "Don't say anything about Jews," she once whispered, as we drew near the rough kennel of a gaunt yellow cur; "he don't know any other religion; he's been with them all his days. I took him after Miss Levy died. He set everything by the family, and I don't want him to think we disapprove of their beliefs."

"I suppose I need not ask you," I said, one day, "with your views of animals and their being like folks, if you think there's a future for them after death?"

To my surprise, the old woman shook her head sadly, and the soft brown eyes grew moist. "No," she said, in a low, mournful voice, "I'm afraid there's no chance of that. I've give it up. I did hold to it as long as I could, and it 'most broke my heart to let it go. But so many of the folks I look up to tell me it isn't so that I've had to give up that p'int. Even Elder Peters, that's so fond of dogs and horses himself, he always said there wasn't any chance of meeting them anywhere in the next world; and Dr. Church held that too;

and good old Mis' Holcombe, that left money
to take care of destitute cats.   They was all
one way, proved it from the Scriptures, you
know—'like the beasts that perish,' and all
that.   They all say there ain't a single word
in the Bible that gives them a reasonable
hope.   There's most everything else spoke of
as being there—folks and angels and martyrs
and saints and trees and flowers and fruit
and streams and precious stones.   But nothing about creatur's, except—well, sometimes
I think there's a chance for white horses—
just a chance."

"For white horses!" I exclaimed, in amaze-
ment.

"Yes; in Revelation, speaking about heaven
and the saints, it tells about their being dressed in white robes and riding on white horses.
But there's another—a dreadful verse in that
book—I never like to think of it.   After telling all the beautiful things that's inside of
heaven, it says, ' But without are dogs.'   Now
ain't that a terrible mournful pictur'?   It's
as if the other animals all give up when they
was told there wasn't any place for them up
there, and just died for good, instincts and all

—if you don't want to call them souls—but dogs, why, they just couldn't do it ; they must follow on after their masters, room or no room. And so I always seem to see them hanging about the door, waiting and waiting, getting a peek in when it opens to let some- body go inside, and maybe catching sight of their masters—oh ! I can't stand it, anyhow. I wish it wasn't writ there, 'Without are dogs.' "

In vain I tried to show the poor woman that the dog of Revelation, banished from bliss with murderers, idolaters, and others of the wicked, was not one of her four-footed friends. She had looked at the harrowing vision too long to be able to banish it at once.

" But there's one thing I won't give in to," she said, " and that is that Scriptur' don't go to show that folks 'd oughter be kind and merciful to creatur's. It does—I say it does. There's heaps and heaps of things that shows it. Of course there's that one about the right- eous man regarding the life of his beast ; but then some might say that was because he needed the beast and wanted its work. But

there's lots of passages besides that. Why,
how beautiful it always speaks about sheep
and lambs! There ain't anything better it
can find to liken God to than a shepherd, and
the tenderest kind of one, too. Why, it says
He gathers the lambs up in His arms and car-
ries them in His bosom; it tells how He makes
them lay down in green pastures, and leads
them out beside the still waters. And the
Master, too, He calls Himself the Good Shepherd, and then explains to the folks what a
good shepherd is, and how he has names for
all his sheep and knows them all, and how
they'll follow him all about and know his
voice. And it says that he'll even give his
own life for his sheep — any good shepherd
will, he sets so much by them. It stands to
reason no one could treat sheep and lambs
cruel anyway if they think much of the Bible.
And telling people not to aggravate the oxen
by muzzling them up while they're threshing
out the corn, and not to do such an unnat'ral,
cruel kind of thing as to seethe a kid in its
mother's milk. And where it tells you in case
you come across a bird's-nest on the ground
or up in a tree, with the mother-bird setting

on her eggs or cuddling her young ones, to be
sure and not hurt her, but let her go. And
the talking so much about creatur's, how
smart and how knowing, and how quick and
how busy, and how bold and how handsome !
There's Solomon, he can't say enough about
the ants being so forehanded and laying up
their food, and the conies building in the
rocks, and the greyhound, which is so ' come-
ly in going.' And in Job it goes on about the
fine looks and the strength and the high spirit
of horses, pawing the ground and smelling the
battle, and all. And I'm sure our Master when
He was here loved the birds, and talked about
them, and spoke of His Father's feeding them
and keeping count of the sparrows. And He
said, however strict folks was about keeping
Sunday, any one would help a creatur' that
fell into a hole, or got hurt any way, that day
or any other. Oh, I tell ye the whole gist of
Scriptur's that way, to my thinking, even if
it don't say up and down in big capitals,
' Don't beat your horses or kick your dogs.'
And Solomon says one real smart thing about
my idee of there not being so much difference,
after all, 'twixt folks and creatur's. Wait a

minute, and let me get the old Bible and read it to you. Here, now : 'For that which be-falleth the sons of men befalleth beasts; even one thing befalleth them ; as the one dieth, so dieth the other ; yea, they have all one breath ; so that a man hath no pre-eminence above a beast,' and so on. Ain't that good? And him so wise, you know !"

"It must be a sad thought," I said to her once, "that you will never see these animal friends in the next world." It was a cruel thing to say, under the circumstances, but I did not stop to think.

A mist clouded the soft, dog-like brown eyes, as they met mine for an instant and then turned quickly away. "It's dreadful," she said, in a low, hushed tone—"dreadful. It's wicked, I know, to say so, but—I couldn't be happy up there and them outside. Me and all the real folks, that's had everything in this world — rights, and laws to protect their rights, and—and—souls—us all inside heaven, and them that's been put upon and worried and tortur'd all their days, them out-side of it all, oh, I couldn't stand it—I know I couldn't ! So—well — maybe I sha'n't be there myself." She went on hurriedly, as if in response to some expression she thought my face might wear : "Not that I'm giving up my religion. That's a sight of comfort to me—more'n anything else, I guess. But, you see, folks generally are so busy saving their own souls and other people's—heathen's and all — they can't attend to righting the awful wrongs done to creatur's, and it's nat-'ral, I know. But I've got a leaning that way, and I'm so made I seem to know how to help animals and coax folks to be good to them. So I just tell God right out all about it—that I feel I must give up my whole life, day in and day out, to helping and comforting these creatur's He's made, and made so like folks in everything but just not having souls. And I tell Him "—she spoke softly and reverently—"I tell Him I love Him and want to serve Him, and I'm on his side, and will be to my dying day. But I've got such a terrible aching and burning over the things done to these creatur's that I can't attend to the other things folks tell me is the highest, most important ones. I haven't got time for all the meetings—the sewing society and

missionary concerts and temperance meetings and teachers' meetings and the anti-
smoking society, and all those stated means,
as they call them. I'm drove day and night,
looking up suffering creatur's, fetching home
them that's lost, nursing the sick, chirking
up the lonesome and homesick. Why, you
wouldn't believe how full my hands be. And
so I tell Him plain, but humble and respect-
ful, that if He thinks best to say, because I
give up the work and duty of a professor, I
must give up the rewards too, why, I've
nothing to say. He knows best, understanding the whole case, and I know He'll do
right. So I just go on with what I've got
to do for these poor things as if I was just
one of them, soul lacking and all. And they
think I am."

I told you I had no story, nothing but a
picture—poorly drawn, I know—of one woman and her work and ways. I do not even
point a moral. Maybe there is none. It is
for you to say.

DAVY'S CHRISTMAS

DAVY'S CHRISTMAS

YES, ma'am, of course I'll tell you, as well as I know how, but there ain't much to tell. As for the change you say 's come over Anderson, why, 'twasn't me that done that, you know.

You see, I was raised where they set a good deal by Christmas — the real part of it, I mean. All the children knew what it was kept for, and whose birthday 'twas, and why folks give presents that day. And we hung up our stockings at home, and had a tree for the Sunday-school, and carols and texts, and all that. Somehow I never knew, or, anyway, stopped to think, about there being other places where nobody done this, nor took any notice of Christmas at all. So, when we moved way out West to Anderson that fall, and I begun to look ahead and lay plans what I should do for Christmas, 'twas a big surprise to me to find none of the boys and girls knew what I was driving at.

'Twas a little place, anyway, you know, and there wa'n't many young folks. There wasn't a church or a Sunday-school there neither ; but somehow that didn't seem to trouble me so much at first as the other thing — that they didn't have any Christmas. You see, I'd had it all my life, and I thought 'twas just beautiful. Why, 'twas almost everything, or, 't any rate, the beginning of everything. So I thought and thought about it, and when I'd got things a little straightened out in my head, I went to mother. You know mother, so I needn't tell you how good she was about it, nor how she entered right into it with me. That's her way — ain't it, ma'am? She always enters into things so when you want her to. And she talked to father for me—that's one good thing about mothers, their talking to your fathers for you — and he come into it too. We was going to have a Christmas, a real one, for the folks there in Anderson.

Now we wa'n't rich, you know that ; but

we was pretty well to do, and we had a nice little home fitted up with all our things from the old place. I'd fetched along my books and cards and maps and pictur's, and the carols we used to sing; and I had some of the things we used to dress the Christmas-tree with—bright little balls and shiny stuff and little bits of candles—so we could have a tree, and there hadn't anybody there ever see one. Mother had her melodeon, and she said she'd play the carols, and we'd all sing 'em together. And father, he promised to talk a little to the folks about the day, and what it meant to everybody. We meant to give presents too—just little cheap ones, o' course, but something, anyway, to every single boy and girl there.

You bet I did enjoy getting up that thing! I tell you, 'twas fun keeping it so secret, and thinking how surprised they'd be, and all. Father and mother helped, but I done most of it myself; for father had his regular work to do, and mother had the baby to 'tend to— little Joshua, you know.

But 'twas all ready at last. I'd picked out a real pretty little tree up on the hill, and father'd cut it down for me, and there 'twas now, standing up in the best room, all shiny with gilt and silver paper, and the little tin balls of different colors swinging on the branches. And there was red apples and pine cones, and the little candles from home all ready to light. 'Twas dreadful pretty. There was little presents for 'em all, mostly things that I'd had give to me Christmases and birthdays, and so on : books and pictur'-cards, and one or two little games, things I was glad enough to give away to them that had so little. So you see what a splendid Christmas 'twas going to be—just the thing to show 'em what it meant, and make 'em always keep it afterwards, some way or 'nother.

Oh, dear me ! It's three whole years ago now, but it 'most makes me cry to think what happened, and how 'twas all, every single bit of that beautiful plan, spoiled ! It's too dreadful to say much about. The folks was to come Christmas Eve for the treat, and just the night before that, the twenty-third of December, our house catched fire and burnt up. Every single thing was burnt, except the clothes we put on in a hurry, and we just saved our own lives—that was about all. As it was, poor father got hurt real bad trying to save things. His hands and arms was all blistered and burnt, and his face scorched; and mother, she catched a dreadful cold, and 'most lost her voice. At first I couldn't think of anything but the house and our furniture and things, and of poor father, and how glad I was we was all alive—mother, and little Joshua, and all. But after a spell it come over me all of a sudden—Christmas, and the time we'd been going to have for the folks! The tree and everything on it was burnt up. The house and best room, where the company was to be, the melodeon, and even the singing-books that had the carols in 'em—everything, every single thing—was gone; even the barn, and Jack, our dear old horse, went, too. Only the cow-house, that stood by itself a little ways off, didn't burn, and our little Jersey cows, Whitefoot and Buttercup, was saved—that was better than nothing.

It had been a house once where folks lived, but it got old and shackly. and some of it tumbled down, and the rest of it made a good place for the cows. There was a fireplace and a chimney to it, so we had a place to go to, such as 'twas. The people round there was all pretty poor, and nobody lived very near by. They asked us to come, and was pleasant enough about it, but we thought we hadn't better do it as long as we could take care of ourselves. So we settled down that night as well's we could in the cow-house, with a big fire to keep us warm, and some blankets and things the folks lent us.

Next morning, the very day before Christmas, you know, just as quick as I got a chance to talk with mother, I had to let it all out. I wasn't as big then as I be now, and I couldn't to save my life keep from crying like a baby when I spoke about the Christmas. I kept saying how could God have done such a thing, when we was just a-going to learn the Anderson folks about the birthday, and what it all meant. "Oh!" I says, "how could He do it?" Well, mother she entered into it—her way, you know! She let me see she allowed for my being disapp'inted, but she said she knew I'd come round to seeing 'twas all right, somehow, if He'd done it ; and she said He didn't need us nor anybody else to learn the Anderson folks about Christmas ; He could show 'em Himself if 'twas best for 'em to know.   And she said I must be a good boy, and give it up, and mebbe next year I'd have another chance. I tried to be good, so's not to trouble her; I helped her with father and little Joshua, and tried to make things comfortable.   But I was thinking and thinking all day about the folks, and how they'd got to wait a whole long year to see what Christmas was.   Come along towards noon I says to mother, couldn't I see if some one wouldn't let me have one of their rooms, and maybe their melodeon, and some of the people help me a little, and have just some sort of a Christmas time, if we couldn't have the tree and the presents.   And she said I could try if I was set on it.   But 'twasn't any good. Folks was willing to come to a treat, but they wouldn't help get it up.   I even went to the little tavern at the Corners, but they said 'twas full that night, and they couldn't be bothered.

I went home—if you could call it home—

and I set down on the floor, and laid my head down on mother's lap—she's got such a nice lap—and told her all about it. She was real good, but she didn't know how to help me. She see herself I'd got to give the whole thing up. But she whispers to me, stroking my head, says she, "Tell God all about it, Davy." So I done it right there, just as I was, with my head in mother's lap. When I got up, I says, "Well, mother, I've got to give it up, and I'm going to stand it like a man. But mebbe," I says, "some of the folks will come anyway — them that lives a good ways off, and hasn't heard about the fire." And she says, "Well, if they do, Davy, we'll be glad to see 'em, though this isn't much of a place to have company."

What do you think? Come evening, if the boys and girls, and the growed folks too, didn't begin to come along! You see, I'd invited 'em some days afore, and hadn't took back the invitations. And I s'pose, even if they knew we didn't expect 'em, they was cur'us to see what we'd do, and to look at the burnt house and all. Why, most everybody round there come, seems to me! 'Twas a real nice night; there wasn't any moon, but I never see the stars shining brighter. I rec'-lect that, 'cause father'd been telling me about the stars that winter, and I'd took to noticing 'em. And as I come in that night I looked up, and see how bright they was, par-tic'lar one big one father called the evening star.

The folks didn't come in at first. They kind of stood round outside, and when I went out to speak to 'em, they said they didn't want to trouble us, but they was round that way, and they thought they'd just see if they could do anything for us. 'Twas pretty cold, and I couldn't bear to see 'em standing out-doors so long. So I run back inside, and asked mother if I couldn't bring 'em in. There wasn't any seats, to be sure, but 'twas warm, and it seemed politer, anyway. Mother said o' course I could; let 'em come in; she didn't mind.

They was a little backward at first, 'peared to feel a mite bashful. But bime-by one after 'nother stepped inside. I felt a little foolish myself, and didn't know just what to say first off. But Jim Bissell, a rough sort of boy from the Corners, he begun to laugh, and says out loud, "Where's your Chris'mus, as you call it, Dave? What's it all about, anyway?"

And then—I don't know to this day how I ever picked up courage for it, but it come into my head I just must tell 'em something, if 'twas only the leastest bit, about the day that was coming to-morrow—I just shet up my eyes one second, and then I wet my lips, and begun. I told 'em what I'd meant to do, and how 'twas all spoiled, and how dreadful sorry I was. I said I'd tried to get some other place to hold the meeting in, but I couldn't, and I'd tried the tavern at the Corners, but there wasn't any room for it there. And then I put it 's well 's I could, about how father was laid up and couldn't talk to 'em, and that I wasn't big enough to explain things myself. "But," I says, "I can read you about it, only I ain't no great of a reader." And then comes over me, all of a sudden, that our Bibles was all burnt up. It just seemed as if 'twas meant them folks shouldn't learn about Christmas that year, and I'd better give up.

But mother says in a softly voice—she was

just back of me—she says, "Don't you know
some verses, Davy?" I knew I did, for I'd
said 'em at a Christmas-tree the year afore.
So I begun: "Now when Jesus was born in
Bethlehem of Judea"—you know how it
goes. At first Jim Bissell laughed, and some
of the others j'ined in, and whispered and
made fun. But the others stopped 'em, and
in a minute I see 'twas dreadful still, and
only just my voice, pretty shaky, you know,
going on with that chapter. I didn't know
only the first 'leven verses. When I come
to the last one—" And when they were come
into the house, they saw the young child and
Mary his mother "—I heard a little gurglin'
sound. I didn't dast to turn my head, but I
knew 'twas little Joshua taking notice. And
just then I heard another queer noise, kind
of a choky noise that was, and I see 'twas
Cap'n Frink, the man they called the wildest
feller about Anderson, though he come from
New England, and was raised, I've heard,
'mongst real good people. There was something the matter with his throat, and he was
coughing till the water come into his eyes,
and that interrupted me a mite. But in a

minute I went over to Luke, and I says that
part about the shepherds and the Baby laying in the manger, on account of there not
being any room in the inn, you know. Then
I stopped, and I thinks to myself, oh, if I
only had the melodeon, and the books with
the carols !

Just then mother says, softly again, " Can't
you sing baby's hymn, Davy ?" Now I 'ain't
got much ear for music, they say, and I was
that scared my voice was croakier than common. I can't turn many tunes, but that one
turns itself, I've heard it so many times from
mother when she was holding little Joshua.
I used to pick it out with one finger on the
melodeon. I says to myself, " Here goes, 't
any rate," and I let out :

"Hush, my dear, lie still and slumber."

'Twas kind of dreadful to hear my own
voice, and nobody j'ining in to help me, and
I got scarier and shakier, till I was just going to break down, when all of a sudden
I found some one was helping. There was
a real nice, loud, sweet voice singing the
words with me, and carrying the tune all

right, only shaking a mite, just as mine done.
And, of all the folks there, who should it be
but Lucy Ann Wells, the roughest woman in
the whole place, that 'most everybody was
afraid of! She had a cross, sharp voice when
she talked, but 'twas real sweet and clear and
pleasant-sounding now. I don't see how she
ever knew that hymn, but she did, and she
and me sung it right along as far as I knew
the words. When we got to where it says:

> "When His birthplace was a stable,
> And His softest bed was hay,"

I see that all the people was looking right
over my head, and kind of behind me, and not
at me at all. So when we ended up, Lucy Ann
and me, and I dast to turn round, I done it.

There wa'n't anything uncommon there—
just mother and the baby. She'd been a-
holding him, and he'd heard us singing his
fav'rite hymn, that he went to sleep by regular, and he'd thought 'twas bedtime, so he'd
dropped off, and mother'd laid him down.

O' course there wa'n't any place to lay him
but the hay. But that was real soft and comfortable, and he did look real cute laying

there, with his pretty yeller hair all fuzzy round his little head, and mother, with her nice, dear, mothery face, a leaning over him.

Seems 's if there ain't much more to tell. To this day I don't get it through my head why they begun to have Christmases themselves, after that, there in Anderson. If I'd 'a' carried out my plan, and had that tree and all, why, I could see how it come about. But when we didn't have any Christmas at all that year—no tree, no presents, no refreshments, no nothing—well, as I said afore, it beats me how they come to keep Christmas the very next year, and ever sence.

CLAVIS

CLAVIS

PERHAPS the child's mother might have found it out sooner than I did if she had lived. I cannot tell. I know she could not have loved the little one more tenderly, watched her more closely. From the hour when I took the child into my arms, out of whose clasp the mother had just slipped away quietly and forever, the little girl was all the world to me.

There was a strange and wonderful sympathy between us two. She understood me always when no one else could, and she told me so. That this comprehension was not gained through the ear, expressed by the tongue, I did not for a long time notice. We lived so quietly, you see, far away from the busy world, in the very heart of nature, among trees and hills and streams, with birds and flowers and wild free things, and we did not talk much. When I held her close to my heart and we looked out upon the shining river, up to the purple hills, into the rosy clouds, or over to the dark, deep forest, there was no need of words. And when there came the rushing sound of the wind among the trees, the music of the brook whose white waters ran over the stones, the glad song of the bobolink, or the tender strain of the thrush, I looked into her deep, still eyes and felt that we were both listening, and that we both heard.

We had no neighbors, few friends, and for a long time there was no one to tell me of anything the child lacked or missed. But there came a time when it was said that my little child did not hear, that her ears were sealed to all sound, and that she would never speak to me.

I do not remember that even then it was a great grief to hear this. Even then, when she was so small, so young, I felt that, silent and deaf to others though she might be, yet she understood me well, and could tell me so. I do not know how this was; I cannot explain it. I know only that I, who had failed hitherto to make my meaning clear to those around me, found comprehension, full understanding, perfect sympathy, in my little silent child.

I had always been a shy, awkward, reticent man. A strange, sad, loveless boyhood, a youth of struggle unrewarded, privation unpitied, longing for affection unsatisfied, had made me this. And now, just when I had ceased to expect it, there came to me all I had needed, craved, despaired of so long. There had always been a strange thing in my life which no one understood or cared for. From my earliest years there had been a constant wonder in my mind, a strange, eager questioning about the meaning of things. I did not care for the answers men give to such questions—for the explanations found in learned books or the wisdom taught in schools. All my life long I had known that there was one key to all the mysteries of which this world is so full, but that no man had ever found it.

I had felt sure that if any one could learn the meaning of just one simple thing in the woods, or on the hills, or among the flowers or birds, he would understand everything; there would be no more puzzles, nothing hidden or unexplained, and from my boyhood I had striven, thirsted, to find that key. Many, many times I had seemed to almost grasp it. Some sight, some sound, some faint elusive odor, would give a hint, a suggestion, and quick, sudden as the flight of a darting bird, the truth I had sought so long would flash before me and was gone. There were so many things to wonder at even in the simple life which my little girl and I lived, and we were always wondering.

Perhaps to you there are no mysteries in the wild flowers. They are so simple, so fair, seen at a glance, passed by, or gathered and thrown aside. But to us there were such strange puzzles there. In the spring, when the little linnæa crept over the ground and lifted its pink bells on slender hair-like stems, there came to us from it always the same fragrance, a subtle perfume we could not define. We were sure no other blossom, no other thing on earth, held that odor ; and yet it brought us memories, was linked with some-

thing we could not recall; it was full of asso-
ciation, but with what? Where had we ever
before breathed that aroma of spice, of sweetness, that it should bring us that strange
feeling—half sadness, half joy, a memory so
like a hope?

And the colors of the flowers—they surely
held a meaning if we could but catch it. The
speedwell's gentle blue, the bear-plum's pale
yellow, the buttercup's polished gold, the
aster's lavender and mauve and purple, the
cardinal-flower's vivid red, the crimson pink
of the wild rose — we knew them all, and
almost understood them. One touch, one
word, to help us, and the whole world of
color would fall into harmony. I think my
little girl understood these flower tints better than I did; perhaps because she did not
hear or speak as others hear and speak her
eyes saw more than most, and she would
hold a brightly tinted blossom and gaze into
its blue or pink or yellow with such deep
content in her strange eyes that I felt she
was learning much of the meaning it held.

But she did not know all. One summer she
had been day after day among the cardinal-

flowers by the brook. She had bent over them and touched them, drinking in the warmth and glow of their brilliant red till she seemed to comprehend all, and to know why these flowers alone held such living fire. But one hot August noon when she was among them, watching them burn to more vivid crimson under the sun's fierce heat, she found, among the others, a stalk of pure white blossoms. They were cardinal-flowers, too, but pale and cold. She led me to the place and showed me the delicate snowy flowers, with a look on her face half sad, half frightened, and very wistful. I could not help her. How could it be? What was the meaning? It was the warmth, the glow, the depth and vividness, which made the other blossoms cardinal-flowers. But here was one which lacked all these qualities, and was like snow, not fire. Never again did my child tell me that she knew the meaning of the cardinal-flower.

And there was a certain plant which always grew in the forest, under the pines, and bore one large rose-colored blossom, just one solitary pouch-like flower upon each slender stalk, always alone, always by itself; we knew it by its oneness, its being single and solitary. One day we found among the rest a plant just the same but that its slender stalk bore two twin blossoms, and they were white, not pink.

But I think there was no puzzle among the flowers so hard to solve as that of the closed gentian. No one could help wondering over that. Why, if it is never to unfold, if no sunshine or dew or soft warm air can ever open its fast-closed petals — why should it be so fair within? For we had looked inside, gently opening the dark purple-blue, bud-like blossom. It was quite finished within, tinted and veined, satin-smooth, as dainty and complete as any of its sisters who open their eyes to the light and air. We could find no secret there, no reason for the shut-up, lonely life, and while I thought and queried and surmised, I could see the wonder grow and deepen in my little voiceless child's tender eyes of darkest blue. But no one helped us; nothing told us the meaning of it all.

The birds made us wonder too. We could

not understand their songs, though each had
its meaning; we were sure of that. For she
heard them too. Sealed as her ears might
be, she felt the notes in some strange unexplained way, and I read them over again in
her eyes. The clear, sweet, far-reaching
whistle of the white-throat sparrow, the soft,
gentle whisper of the waxwing, the swamp-
sparrow's trill, the plaintive cry of the wood-
pewee, the glad, free strain of the bobolink,
the gurgle and croon of the cuckoo—we knew
them all. But why did each bring such a different thought? There was one small bird
whose color was like that of the dark pine-
trees where he sang, and his strain was almost like human speech, always the same—
just a few appealing words, then silence. Up
on the hill above the lake the winter-wren
sang. There were so many different mean-
ings in his song, bright and sad and tender.
We smiled as we heard it, but the tears were
very near our eyes. And in early morning
and in the twilight the veery always rang his
silver bells. Over and over again they rang
and vibrated, till our hearts ached with the
sweetness and mystery of it. Why did the

bird sing that strain and never any other?
And what did it mean?

And there was the hermit-thrush. I have
said that there were many things which
seemed at times about to give us the light we
sought. But of all these the song of the
hermit - thrush most often brought us such
glimpses. In the evening twilight of a June
day, when all nature seemed resting in quiet,
the liquid, melting, lingering notes of the solitary bird would steal out upon the air and
move us strangely. What was the feeling it
awoke in our hearts? Was it sorrow or joy,
fear or hope, memory or expectation? And
while we listened, my little quiet girl and I,
suddenly we would turn with quick, eager
looks and read in each other's eyes the same
thought. The meaning of it all—it was coming; we should know; it was trembling on
the air, and in an instant it would reach us.
Then it faded, it was gone, and we could not
even remember what it had been.

The name of my child was Clavis. When
I had first looked into her deep, earnest eyes
of violet-blue there had arisen in my heart a
strange hope that through this little girl)

might find the meaning, the key, I had sought so long, and in that hope I gave her this name. As the years went by, hope became expectation, expectation foreknowledge, and I knew that sooner or later my silent child would bring me the truth.

I do not know just how it came about, but many people learned of this strange questioning of ours. I sought no knowledge, no help, in the matter from others, even from the most learned men. For I had read their books, and I knew they themselves had never found the key. But they came to me from far and near, and each one brought his own explanation, his own theory or creed. I will own that sometimes — for they were very learned men—their words half satisfied me, and for a moment I felt that I had grasped the clew I sought. But always, always when I turned and met the quiet eyes of my child, I saw in their dark-blue depths the certainty that I had but touched the surface of things, and that far, far below lay the truth I was seeking.

There was a strange thing about these meetings. However earnest and enthusiastic the man might be who came to expound his own belief and teach us the meaning of things, I always saw a change come over him before he went away. For when he looked into my child's quiet eyes, so deep, so full of hidden meaning, his own eyes were troubled, his looks confused; his voice lost its self-confident ring; his words came more slowly and with hesitation, and sometimes ceased utterly. Such a one would sometimes tell us before he went away that perhaps, after all, he had not discovered the real meaning of things : perhaps the key was yet to be sought and found.

So the months and years went by, and more and more often came to us both those faint brief glimpses of a great satisfying truth, of one single simple key which should unlock all our mysteries. There were mountains about our home, and strange things happened upon those hills. Sometimes when the summer sun lay hot and bright upon them we saw shadows upon their peaks and sides. Some were shadows of clouds which floated above them ; these we saw and recognized. But there were other shadows there,

strange, unfamiliar things, like nothing in
the sky, like nothing on the earth, wonderful shapes and full of meaning. As I clasped
my little Clavis's hand tightly and we gazed
eagerly, tremblingly, upon those dark roll-
ing shades cast there by something we could
not see, of which we knew nothing, we felt
the whole truth very near. There is a wonderful light that comes sometimes at evening upon those hills, creeping from base to
summit, changing from pink to purple, from
purple to blood-red, till all is fire and glow
and glory, and every time it came it flashed
a quick, fleeting hint of what we sought.
And never, never did the hermit-thrush
chant his silver, melting, throbbing, ringing
strain without our seeming to hold for one
short, vanishing instant the key to all things.
If it could but sing always, we thought, or
even a little longer, we should know all.

The learned men, the great scholars, think-
ers, writers, came more often to us. I do
not remember how it happened that at last
these many great men agreed to assemble
together at our home — my little girl's and
mine — and listen to what we should say to

them. They knew well, for we had told them so, that we had never yet found the one password, the true solution, the right key to all the strange things about us. But I think they wished to be convinced that any one key would open all, that there was but one solution to all problems, one answer to all riddles, as I believed, and as Clavis knew. And I talked to them. It was early June and in the evening twilight, and we were out-of-doors. It seems strange to me, as it doubt-less does to you, that so many great men came together there to listen to one unsatis-fied, questioning man and one little, silent, expectant girl. But they came, and under the shadow of the mighty hills they gathered there, and I stood in their midst, with Clavis at my side. I cannot tell you what we said to them: because of all that came after-wards, I forget much. I know that we spoke of the strange mysteries about us even there in that quiet spot, among the dark pines and under the shadow of the mountains. Then I told them, and Clavis said it over and over again in that silent way I cannot make you comprehend, that we felt sure that there was one single clew to all these riddles, if we could but find it. The secret of the flower that never opens, like a bud, an undeveloped, immature, unfinished thing to outward seeming, but a fair, complete blossom within ; the meaning of the purple light that comes upon the hills at evening ; the suggestion in the perfume of the linnæa ; the memories — or hopes—awakened by the thrush's song ; the black shadows on the sunny mountain-side, cast there by something far above, which our eyes cannot see ; the frost - white cardinal-flower springing up among its glowing sisters ; the large pink blossom in the forest, whose very nature and property seems to be that it should be solitary on its slender stem, yet bearing sometimes fair twin flowers—all these things, and many more which made us wonder and question now, would lie open, plain, and simple before us could we touch the key we sought. We told them how near it sometimes came to us—how a perfume, a sight, a sound, a touch, seemed so close to bringing the clew. And I saw, and my little girl's eyes shone with a glad but still light as she saw it too, that one after another remembered how such moments, such glimpses, had come to him, and how brief, how sweet, how fleeting, they had been. While I talked, the breeze that always comes down at sunset from the cool mountains sprang up, and as it reached me it brought that strange, elusive odor of spice, of sweetness, from the pink bells of the linnæa growing thickly among the pine-trees, and for one brief, sudden instant I remembered or foresaw its meaning. Then, like the faint, evanescent perfume itself, the thought was gone, and I could not recall or tell it. I looked at Clavis. She too had read that meaning, but it had vanished; yet her deep eyes shone with a still, glad light, which said that it would surely come again, and we should keep it.

Now the wonderful light crept up the hills. It was golden at first, and turned the grass and the tree trunks yellow and russet, then it changed the leaves overhead to orange, and then flushed and reddened as it crept up the hill-sides, crimsoning the lower peaks, and still rising, rising, till, as it touched the top of the highest, grandest mountain, it made its rugged, rocky summit as red as blood.

Suddenly all my being was flooded with a quick, glowing flame which showed me all we were seeking. For the instant I knew it; I could tell it to the people. But before my slow tongue could form the words the color upon the hill-tops faded, the flush died away, and I had forgotten. I turned an almost hopeless, despairing look upon my little girl. She was very still, as always. But upon her soft cheek lingered the flush of rose which had left the sky, and in her quiet eyes there shone an almost triumphant light which spoke of victory very near. They saw it too, and clustered close together and around us, while over all came that hush which seems to throb with expectancy and thrill with anticipation.

Up in a lofty pine above our heads a little lonely bird uttered his simple strain—a few appealing, wistful notes, then silence. Then a veery rang his silver bells. Over and again they rang and vibrated, till our hearts ached with the sweetness and mystery of it.

Then from the hill-side across the river a hermit - thrush began to sing. Everything besides was very still, and the air throbbed

and trembled, pulsated and quivered with
that wonderful strain. And I knew all : I
held the key. A moment of suspense, of
waiting, fearing lest it vanish as had died
into silence the bird's song, then I looked into
my child's eyes. Yes, she knew it too. I
read it over again in the dark depths of her
eyes, and the strange, sweet, mysterious smile
that lingered about her silent lips.

Then I spoke. For the first time in all the
ages was told the secret of things. I held
the key, and I showed it to them all. I cannot tell you of that hour, the wonder, the ex-
ultation, the glad surprise ; no words could
make you comprehend. It was my voice
that spoke, but it was at Clavis that they
looked, and from her stillness they gathered
more than from my spoken words.

Then hands clasped hands, eyes gazed into
each other, lips quivered, cheeks were wet
with tears. They knew all now, and it was
all so simple, learned in one brief second.
How had we missed it so long, sought it so
vainly ? How could there have been any key
but this, now ours forever ? No, I say again,
I cannot tell you of it. In all time there

never was an hour like that. Will ever such a one come again ?

Darkness came on, the breeze from the mountains grew chill, and we must separate. On the morrow we would meet again, and then decide how this great news might be told to the world. When all had gone, and my little girl and I were left alone, I took her to my heart, and we talked in our strange, silent way of what had come to us. I was full of a solemn, awed wonder, but she felt no surprise, only a still joy that what she had known was coming should be here now. I had thought that the excitement and wonder would banish sleep from my eyes, but I slept long and dreamlessly. I awoke to dark skies, thick clouds, and a chill air. By degrees I remembered. I thought of the assembly of the night before, of the questioning looks, the earnest faces upturned to mine, of the purple light, the linnæa's fragrance, the lonesome bird in the pine-tree, then the hermit-thrush's song. I saw the glad, the solemn, exulting faces, recalled the joy, the peace, the wonder of those to whom the key was shown. But—what was that key ? For an instant I had lost it as in the old days. But it would return ; never could such a blessed thing as came to me that fair June evening and stayed so long—never in life could it be forgotten, lost. I was but half awake ; I was yet dazed with sleep ; I would go out into the morning air, look up at the hills, and remember all. But I could not grasp it ; it just escaped each time I sought to seize it. Like the vanishing perfume of a flower, the fading light upon the hills, a bird's faint dying song, it drifted from me.

But I was not afraid. So many knew it now, it could not be lost. While I stood in the raw chill air of the dark morning, one of the learned men who had been with us the night before came to me. His face was a little troubled, but brightened as he saw me, and he spoke quickly, eagerly. He told me that in his sleep the clear outlines of that wonderful truth he had held the last night had become somewhat blurred, confused. Would I tell him again, now in the light of day, just what had brought such joy, such peace, when he first heard it ? For the moment I could not tell him, and I said so.

One after another came to us those who had
listened and heard and rejoiced a few hours
before, and all with the same troubled confusion. Was it so with all? Had we let sleep
steal away that wonderful, priceless treasure?
So it seemed; for all came, and all had forgotten. For a brief instant I was seized with
a terrible fear. Then I smiled, and remembered there was no cause for alarm : Clavis
knew all; Clavis never forgot, never lost
anything she had once held fast. I went to
her. She was asleep, her fair hair like sunshine about her head, the white lids shut
down over her dark eyes. As I looked at
her she awoke. I need not have been afraid.
One glance into her still glad eyes showed
me she had not forgotten. The key was not
lost : Clavis knew all. She told me in her
silent way, as I took her in my arms, that all
was well : she held the key; we should all
have it—we need not fear ; she knew all, and
we should soon know all likewise. She was
very weary, she said, and would like to rest a
little while—only a little while, and we should
come to her and know all. It was almost
like the hour in which I first held out the key

when I went back to the fearful, trembling men and told them that my little child remembered. Not one doubted ; all believed and were at peace. By-and-bye I went to her again. She was asleep. The white lids lay over her dark, deep eyes, and hid their meaning. But the old, mysterious, all - knowing smile rested about the silent lips, and I was not afraid. Nor am I afraid now. No, though she never wakened. Has she not given me the secret she held?

A TRANSIENT

A TRANSIENT

'Twas when I was keeping the Banks House over to Bentley Centre, more'n thirty year ago. Mr. Harris had been dead quite a spell, and I was running the house alone and doing well. Mother lived with me, but she was too old to do much, and feeble anyway. 'Twas the only tavern in the Centre, and open all the year round, but we didn't have many folks except in summer. But from the last of June 'way into September I had a nice lot of summer boarders every year, and we had a good many transients, stopping over for dinner, and often all night too, with supper and breakfast. There wasn't much to bring business people. You've been there, haven't you? It's just a quiet little place, but it's got the mountains all round it, making it sightly and nice, and plenty of green, cool, woodsy spots to walk or sit in. And that's what summer boarders like.

The transients was most generally folks that was travelling for pleasure through the mountains and on their way to the Gorge or back. Sometimes farmers come along on their way to Westboro' to 'tend the county fair, or horse men for the races, and then again there'd be a runner or two travelling for some city store or other. But the transient you asked me to tell you about—put up to it, as you said, by Dr. Little—was another sort. The first time I saw him—I remember it as well as if 'twas last week—was the summer Mis' Haskins's folks boarded with me. You know they're among the first families, as to standing, in the State, and 'twas a great thing for my house, and for the whole town, for that matter, to have them put up there. Mis' Haskins wasn't well that year, and was dreadful nervous and whimsy. So they thought they'd go to some real quiet kind of place, instead of a big hotel, as they'd generally done. She was pretty hard to please, but I did my best, and she got along well enough, considering. But one day everything appeared to go

wrong, seems 's if. There wasn't any other
boarders that time—'twas the last of June—
but the Haskins folks and the Sperrys from
Derby. And they set all together at meals
to the long table by the south windows,
where 'twas light and airy. There was twelve
of 'em, five each side and one to each end,
and 'twould have held sixteen comfortable.
Well, that day the whole party'd been out
driving in two wagons, over to the east village and Wells Pond. They'd had dinner put
back to half-past one, and 'twas all ready
when they come in. They'd called at Miss
Leonard's on their way home, and brought a
young lady that was boarding there, a friend
of Miss Ellen Sperry's, back with them. I
was in the kitchen, dishing up, when I heerd
'em all trooping in together to the table, and
then the chairs scraping as they pulled 'em
out to set down. Then I heerd a kind of loud
speaking out, and some talking back, and a
sort of fuss, and next moment Sarah Willett,
the table girl, come running out. And she
says, a little flustered, "Mis' Haskins won't
set down and won't let nobody else set down,
'cause there's too many folks to the table."

I knew she'd got it wrong some way, for, as I said before, the table would accommodate sixteen easy, and I went right in. They was all standing up by their chairs, looking real hungry and cross, and Mis' Haskins was talking in a kind of scolding, upset way. "No, I won't do it," she says, "it's a-tempting Providence ; it's as much as my life's worth. No, no, no !" and she begun to sort of cry.

"Why, what's the matter?" says I. "Is anything wrong, Mis' Haskins ?" And then two or three of them spoke up all to once, and I got to understand that there was thirteen to set at that table, and that was bad luck. I don't recollect that I'd ever heerd of that sign before, though I've often read about it late years and seen a few folks that held by it. But it wasn't one of our sayings there in Bentley. Thirteen wasn't any worse than any other number there ; a little better, maybe, for it went by the name of a baker's dozen, and generally meant something thrown in, which is always satisfying in this world. But I see at once 'twas a sign Mis' Haskins believed in, and that she was terrible upset. But what in the world could I do ? They was

all one party and all hungry, and I couldn't
ask any one of them to leave the table, and
there wasn't another boarder in the house to
call in. I was at my wits' end, and didn't
know what I'd better do, when all of a sudden,
but very quiet, a man come into the door
that led out of the front hall and walked
right up to the table. He was an under-size,
homely looking man, but he had a real pleasant kind of face, a mite freckled, and slick,
thinnish red hair—a perfect stranger to me.
Everybody stopped talking and turned to
look at him. He sort of bowed to us all, and
says, in a bashful kind of way but real friendly, "Don't let me put you to any trouble,"
he says; "I'm only a transient for dinner."
Well, I never was so glad to see any one in
all my life. And all the folks was tickled to
death, and showed it. You'd have thought
he'd been a bit surprised at the way they
give him a welcome and made room for him,
but he took it as calm as you please, and
dropped right into the chair Sarah Willett set
for him, without a word.

Sarah said afterwards that he didn't hardly say anything through the meal, but eat

hearty, as if he enjoyed his victuals. Only once, when young Mr. Sperry spoke to him direct and told him what a fix he'd helped 'em out of, and how much they was obleeged to him for happening in, he says, " Don't speak of it; 'tain't anything," and went on with his dinner. I meant to speak to him myself before he got away, but I was kept by one thing and another, and when I got into the office at last, he'd gone. He paid his half-dollar to Parker Smith, who was clerking for us that season, and went off. " Did he have a team," I says to Parker, " or was he afoot ?" And Parker didn't know, hadn't took notice. Well, of course there isn't anything wonderful in that part of the story. 'Twas lucky he happened along just that minute, that's all. And I never should have thought of the man again but for what come after.

'Twas two or three weeks after that, one hot day in July, that I had the biggest scare of my whole life, I believe. Some ways or other I'd turned my ankle, and 'twas swelled up and stiff so's I couldn't put my foot to the floor. I was up in my bedroom, setting in

my rocking-chair, with my foot all wrapped
up with cloths wet with opedildoc and up on
a cricket. All the boarders was off one way
or other, except Mis' Skinner. She was in
her room with Janie, her little girl. After a
spell she come over to my room with her
bonnet on and hold of Janie's hand, and asked
me if she could leave the child there with me
for a few minutes while she went over to the
post - office. "She don't need any looking
after, Mis' Harris," she says. "She'll play
round the room real good and quiet, only I
don't exactly like to leave her all alone." I
always liked children, and Janie was a favorite of mine, so of course I said let her stay.
Well, she trotted around and looked at my
things and played with her dolly. I was
knitting, hard at work on a new kind of bed-
spread with a real mixed-up pattern Miss Lee
had been learning me. I got to the most tick-
lish place in it, where the holes come in, and
I was looking close at it and saying over to
myself, " Put your thread over and knit one,
put your thread over and narrer, knit three
plain," when I heerd a little noise. I looked
up quick, recollecting the child—oh dear,

dear, dear ! My south window was wide
open, and there was a morning-glory vine
climbing up on some strings just outside.
There was pink and blue and white flowers
on it, all shut up and twisted, of course, at
that time o' day, but they looked bright and
pretty to Janie. So she'd climbed up in a
chair and tried to reach 'em. The chair'd
tipped, and she'd slipped out, and—oh ! there
she was hanging with her little white frock
catched on the thing the green blinds fasten
to. Before the dress give way, before I could
holler out, before—oh, anything—I see some
one right in my room step up quick behind
the child, catch her up in his arms, unhitch
her frock, and put her down on the carpet
close up to me. For a spell I didn't think of
anything but Janie and her being safe and
sound. I kept stroking her yellow head as
she leaned it up agin my dress, and I felt
sort of sick and head-swimmy. Then I heerd
the door creak, and when I looked up there
was a man going out. He was an under-size,
homely looking man, with a real pleasant
freckly face and thin reddish hair, and I see
he was the transient that helped us out at

the table that day I was telling about. I called out to him to stop, and begun to pour it all out how thankful and obleeged I was and all, but he only says, very quiet, " Don't speak of it ; 'tain't anything," he says. Then he mumbles out sort of quick and bashful something about how he was passing, and see I needed a little help, and come in. I couldn't hear him very plain, and then he was gone. I couldn't follow him, 'count of my lame foot, and he didn't appear to hear when I called out to him again. So off he went without any more thanks from me or anybody.

Well, that time I did ask a heap of questions about him, but nobody seemed to know a thing. Folks had seen him coming along the street, and Mary Willey see him running like a streak through our front gate and into the house that afternoon. But nobody knew who he was, nor which way he come from or went to.

I disremember just what was the next time I saw him. Mebbe 'twas the day Hiram Merrit's cows broke into our cornfield. There wasn't any men folks about, but Aleck Brace, a little fellow not more'n twelve year old,

was in the barn, and he run out to see if he
could drive 'em out. I knew he couldn't do
it alone, and I was just starting out myself,
though my ankle wasn't strong yet a while,
when I see the cows was all running out o'
the field, and there was a man helping Aleck
drive 'em. I didn't get a chance to speak to
the boy till 'most night, and then I asked
him who it was helped him get the cows out.
He said 'twas a stranger to him, a man that
was going by and see the trouble. Said he
was a smallish man, with slinky red hair and
freckled as a turkey egg, but a real friendly
way with him. I guessed in a minute 'twas
that transient again.

I don't know but 'twas afore that, after all,
that he turned up just at the very minute
the keeping-room chimney got afire. I was
out myself, and there wasn't anybody down-
stairs but Sarah Willett and old Aunty Mills
that was turning and sewing over the breadths
of the carpet, and up-stairs there wasn't any
gentlemen, only two or three of the ladies.
I heerd about it as I was coming up the
street, and I run home as fast as I could. But
when I got there 'twas all out and Sarah was

sweeping up the soot. She said they'd had a dreadful scare, but just 's they was 'most distracted somebody run in and emptied a bag of salt on the fire—'twas only a blaze of papers Sarah 'd been burning to get 'em out of the way—and it put it right out. Neither she nor Aunty Mills had noticed who done it. But Parker Smith, the clerk, come in a spell afterwards, and he says, "I .see that sandy-haired man just now, that was here to dinner the day Mis' Haskins had the tantrums." So I felt certain sure that transient had helped me out again.

'Twas the queerest thing. He never went anywhere else, never give assistance to any of the neighbors, and nobody knew who or what he was. But he was always and forever turning up in the very nick, yes, the nickest of time, when I needed help or got into any scrape or mess. They wasn't all big things he done, some was little; they wasn't all solemn things, some was real comical. Why, once I'd gone over to Petersville with Mis' Bryan to have a pictur' took of her baby. It was fretty with its teeth, and wouldn't look pleasant, all the pictur' man and the rest of us could do. 'Twas getting late, and I'd got to be home to make tea-rusk for supper. I was real nervous, but just then a man come in, or was in, for I didn't see him open the door. He stepped up in front of the baby, just where the pictur' thing couldn't take him, and he begun to move his hands up and down, and wiggle his feet, and shake his head all covered with smooth stringy red hair, and twist his homely, freckled face in such a ridic'lous way that the baby, let alone the rest of us, just laughed right out, and I've got the pictur' of it with the laugh all sot on his little countenance. 'Course 'twas that transient. But he wouldn't stop to say a single word, and was off before we could thank him.

Another time I'd been out in the rain and got wet, and I catched cold. I felt sick all over, and that night I thought I'd take some hot peppermint tea. I went to the closet for the peppermint, and there was the bottle all empty ; not a single drop left. Now if there's a thing I pride myself on, it's my never being out of peppermint. It's the one thing that every respectable family should keep in the house. Aunt Nancy Bartlett used to say that to be without peppermint in the house overnight was temptin' Providence, and I guess she was about right. It's the one thing I know that's hot and cold to the same time. So, nat'rally, it's good for folks that's hot-blooded and feverish, and for people that's peaked and shivery. But there I was without a drop in the house, and late in the evening, too. Just then I thought I heerd a noise at the back of the house. I went to my window and listened, but I couldn't hear anything. Pretty soon I felt sure there was steps in the yard, and all of a sudden I recollected I hadn't bolted the side door. I took a candle and run down-stairs. I looked about a little, and see there wa'n't nothing wrong; then I fastened the door and started to go up-stairs. I don't know what 'twas made me turn round and look at the clock that stood on a little shelf in the entry. Just as I done it I see a bottle standing there by the box of matches, and I reached up and took hold of it. It was a middlin'-size bottle, and 'twas brimful of peppermint right up to the cork, as if it had just come out of Deacon Hubbard's store.

Do you s'pose I didn't know, just as well as if I'd seen him, that 'twas that friendly transient done that?

But I tell you there was another kind of help that man fetched me once, and I'll never forget it to my dying day. I told you mother was living with me then. She was most eighty, and she failed up fast that summer. The hot weather was too much for her, and she grew weaker, and one day in August— 'twas the 25th—we see plain she was a-dying. Dr. More had been and gone, saying she wouldn't last many hours, and there wasn't anything he could do. She hadn't sensed anything all day, and her eyes was shut. I was setting close by her, and Libby States, my niece-in-law, nigh by. There wasn't anybody else in the room. All of a sudden I see ma move her lips as if she was trying to speak, but she didn't open her eyes. I leaned over her and says, " What is it, ma?" She sort of whispers, " Sing 'How—firm—a— foundation'—" and I knew she wanted her favorite hymn. Now I never could sing a note in my life, hadn't any ear or voice or idee of tune, besides being all choky with sorrow now. Libby was crying so hard she couldn't raise a note. I tried to say the hymn over, instead of singing it, but I see that didn't satisfy ma. She'd always been fond of music, sung in the choir when she was young. Her poor dry lips moved again, and she says, "Sing, sing!" Oh dear, what wouldn't I've given to do what she wanted! Just then I heerd a voice begin the old hymn to the old tune, the very one ma wanted. The door was on a jar, and somebody was singing just outside in the entry. 'Twasn't much of a voice; it flatted terribly, and it cracked on every single high note, but it satisfied mother. She sort of smiled, and she kept her thin, wrinkled old hands—is there anything on this whole earth like your mother's hands?—moving a little on the sheet to keep time. The voice went right through the whole hymn—a real long one, you know; and just as it come to

" He'll never, no, never, no, never forsake,"

ma stopped moving her hands, and sort of whispers, " Never — forsake —" and then, "Ann " (that's my name), and a second after

175

she says, very softly, " Nathan," and she was gone.

Nathan was my only brother, a little fellow dead and buried twenty year before, but mother'd never forgot him. I could just remember him — a cute, homely little fellow, with sandy hair that never would curl, and a pleasant little face tanned and freckled with being out-doors. But ma thought there never was such a child, said he was too good to live, always doing things for folks, so helpful and self-denying. She said he was always talking of how he was going to spend his whole life, just helping folks and getting 'em out of trouble, partic'lar his own folks. He died, poor young one ! when he was nine year old ; so he never had much chance to show what a helper he could be. But here was ma thinking of him, and saying his name over the very last thing.

I mustn't make this story too long and tire you all out, so I won't tell you how I felt to lose my mother, and the lonesome time that come afterwards. I found out what I'd felt pretty sure of all the time—that 'twas my friend, the transient, that had come in just the very minute he was needed and sung that hymn for ma. I didn't see him myself, but Sarah Willett met him on the stairs, and knew him right away. I didn't think of anything for a spell but mother and the last things I could do for her. But after the funeral I begun to remember what a comfort the hymn had been to her, and I was bound to find out something about that man. But 'twasn't any good, all my questions and searching out. Nobody knew who he was, or'd ever had any talk with him, though a lot of folks had seen him one time or another, and always pretty close to my house.

'Twas a few weeks after that time, one day in September, that Dr. More stopped at my door in his buggy. He said he was going to see a sick woman over to North Bentley, and as he should have to pass right by the Red Hill burying-ground, where ma was, he thought maybe I'd like to go out there with him. I was glad of the chance, for I hadn't been there since the funeral, and I went up-stairs to put on my things. As I was hurrying, so's not to keep the doctor waiting, I thought to myself that I wished I had some flowers to put on mother's grave. She was a master-hand for flowers, could always make them grow and bloom. And she set a great deal by the wild flowers 'round Bentley, and knew 'em all apart. "It's just the time," I says to myself, "for blind gentian that ma always liked so, and the twisted-stalk and everlastings. And goldenrod and blue daisies is out a plenty. But the doctor 'll be in a hurry, and I can't ask him to stop for me to pick any." I run down-stairs and out to the buggy. Just as I got in, Dr. More handed me a big bunch of posies, and says : "Here's your flowers. I'm glad you had them ready."

"Why, what in the world !" I says. "Where did these come from ?"

Dr. More looked real surprised, and says, "Why, I thought you sent them out ! A man fetched them here to me just now, and says, 'Here's some flowers for Mis' Harris.'"

"What man ?" I says.

"He was a stranger to me," says the doctor, "and I didn't take partic'lar notice of him."

But I knew who 'twas well enough. There

wasn't but one person on the whole airth that would 'a' happened along with just them posies at just that minute. 'Twas that transient again. I looked at the flowers as we rode along. There was blind gentians, purply blue, with their green leaves a mite streaky and spotty. Mother she was from Vermont, and she called them dumb foxgloves. You know what I mean—them flowers that's always buds and never open. And there was a lot of twisted-stalk, the big kind that comes late, with a spike of frosty-looking white flowers that smell just the way a peach-pit tastes. And there was everlastings and goldenrod and blue daisies—all the things ma'd been fond of and I'd been wishing for.

Well, then I just had to tell Dr. More all about it. This last thing had somehow stirred me all up, and I begun to think there was something a good deal out of the common about this man and his doings. I was dreadful excited, and I let the doctor have the whole story. I told him all about it, all the things that had happened to me, and all the times this man had helped me out, and how I couldn't find out anything about him, and couldn't get a word with him, and nobody could, and all that. But, some ways or other, it didn't seem to make much impression on the doctor. He didn't appear to think 'twas no great of a myst'ry, nothing very amazing, after all. I guess I didn't tell it just right, mebbe. 'Tany rate, he said things only'd happened so; he dare say the man was all right, and we'd find out all about him some time. Said he was a respectable - looking man, and pleasant spoken, and he'd surmised at first he was some relative of mine that was staying to my house. I suppose he meant the man favored my family. He said women folks was given to imaginings and such. Dr. More was a single man, and they said he'd been disappointed when he was young.

I disremember how long 'twas before I see the man again, or whether I ever did see him more'n once after that time. But any ways, I recollect the last time, and everything that happened then, as well as if 'twas last week. 'Twas in October, the very beginning of the month. All my boarders had been gone some time. I was doing my own work, for I didn't need any help when I was alone, except Wells Sanford for out-door chores. 'Twas after five o'clock one afternoon I see a team drive up to my door and stop, and there was a wagonful of folks come visiting. They was my relations from Danby, Cousin Levi Bourne's folks — him and his wife, and her mother and Joshua, and his wife and little Abigail. They'd come to have supper and spend the night. I was dreadful glad to see 'em, and made 'em real welcome. I had plenty of things in the house to do with, and I knew I could get 'em up a good supper in no time. But who was going to wait on them at table while I was cooking, frying their griddle-cakes and all? 'Twas kind of chilly that day, and I made 'em all set up to the wood fire in the keeping-room, and I went out to the kitchen to see what I could do. I set to work beating up biscuit and making my batter for the cakes, and chopping up the cold beef and potatoes for hash, when I heerd a man's step in the back entry. Then some one come to the door and looked in. 'Twas kind of dark, and I couldn't see at first, but I heerd a man's voice say, " Don't put yourself out any, Mis'

Harris; it's only a transient for supper," and I knew in one minute 'twas that man.

I was in such a hurry, and so nervy and flustered, that somehow I didn't think of how I'd wanted to see him, and all I wanted to say. But I just says, " Deary me, another for supper, and me with not a soul in the house to help me."

He come in real quiet, set his hat down on the table, and says, very pleasant and soft : " Let me help ye, Mis' Harris. I'm quite a hand to help, I am."

And if you'll believe me, before I could say a word he set to work. He set the table, getting out the crockery without asking me a thing, going in and out very quick and still, laying the napkins around, and putting on the plates and knives and forks. He fixed it real nice, but in a kind of an old-fashioned way. When I went in to take a look at it, I declare it looked for all the world like my mother's tea-table when I was a young one ; all the more because he'd used the old blue and white crockery and some other odd dishes ma'd left to me. He helped me about every single thing ; he was real handy for a man, and saved me lots of steps and trouble. Pretty soon he says, still just as easy and quiet, " I suppose you'd like to have me wait on table," he says. " I'm used to waitin', and there ain't nothin' I like so much as helpin' folks to things." I tell you I was pleased. Seems queer now that I took it so easy and let a man that had come for his own supper work around so, but it seemed to come real nat'ral then. Well, he waited on table, and I never see any one do better, and so they all said. Levi told me afterwards that he waited on them more's if he was a friend doing for 'em than like paid help. He put a big book in one of the chairs for little Abigail to set on, and he lifted her up on it as if he was her pa, and pinned her napkin round her neck just as nice. Old Mis' Fish, Levi's wife's mother, was getting old and sort of childish, and when he passed the biscuit to her she looked up at him, and she says : " How air ye, sir ? Your face is real familiar, but I disremember your name. How do you call yourself ?" she says. " You can call me Nathan," he says, very pleasant and soft.

I didn't hear nor know anything about it

till they told me afterwards. He was real attentive to the old lady, wrapping her knit shawl around her every time it slipped off, and picking up her specs when she dropped 'em. They said he had a real friendly way with him, urging 'em to eat, pressing the victuals on 'em, and doing a good deal more'n there was any call for. Bime-by they finished, and I heerd their chairs scrape, and then they went into the keeping-room again. I run in for a minute to tell 'em I'd be ready pretty soon to visit with 'em, and they begun to ask me about the man that waited on table. Levi said he thought first he might be a relation—he had a kind of family look—and when he told 'em his name was Nathan, he was pretty sure of it, because that had been a great name among the Bourneses for generations. But I told him 'twa'n't so ; the man was 'most a stranger, and I didn't even know till that minute his name was Nathan. But I said that bime-by I'd come in and tell 'em something remarkable about this transient and the time I'd had with him.

Then I went back into the dining-room. The man was there waiting for me, though

I'd been dreadful afraid he'd go off in his aggravating way before I come back. He'd seemed real taken with my old chiny, and he was standing by the table with a piece of it in his hand. 'Twas a queer, old-fashioned thing—a mug—sort of yellowish white, with a black pictur' on it, and it had been my little brother Nathan's; he'd always drunk his milk out of it. He set it down real careful 's I come in, and I says: "Now you and me, we must have our supper. I'll run out and put the griddle on and fry some hot cakes, and I'll be back in a jiffy. But first," I says, "I must know what to call you, for I 'ain't an idee what your name is."

He says, kind of bashful like, "You might call me Nathan."

"But that's your first name, I suppose," I says.

"Yes, ma'am," he says, with a real pleasant look on his face, "that's my very first name."

"And might I ask your last one," I says, "so's to call you by it?"

He waited a minute, and then he says, "You wouldn't know any better if I was to tell you; you wouldn't understand it; but Nathan's my first name."

I thought that was kind of queer, but I only said, "Well, when I bring in your supper we must have a little talk. For you know well enough," I says, smiling, and nodding my head at him, "that there's a good many things to be gone over betwixt you and me, and there's a sight of things I'm beholden to you for, and never a chance before to say obleeged to ye."

"'Tain't worth speaking of, Mis' Harris," he says, in his softly way. "I was dreadful glad to help ye. There ain't nothin' I set by more'n helpin' people, partic'lar my own folks."

"What did he mean by that?" I asks myself, as I fried the griddle-cakes and drawed some fresh tea. "I ain't his folks as I know; mebbe he means his fellow-bein's or his neighbors. I mean to ask him."

But I never done it. He was gone when I went back into the dining-room, and sure's I live and breathe, from that day to this I've never catched a sight of that man—never, never, never. Nobody see him go, but Levi heerd the side door shut, and then steps going down the walk. All my looking and asking and wondering and guessing come to nothing. All I ever knew about him you know yourself now.

Dr. Little, that told you to ask me about it, hasn't been here long. He's dreadful interested in folks' minds and heads—the inside of 'em—and what they believe, and why they believe it, and all that. They've got some name for that sort, but I disremember it; but 'tany rate, he's one. He's made me tell him that story twenty times if he has once, and he goes over 'n' over it with me. He uses pretty big words, but I've got so I can follow him after a fashion. He'll ask me what I really think about it myself. Well, I tell him I don't know; sometimes I think one thing, and sometimes another, and then again I don't think anything at all. Then he asks me if I ever thought that maybe this man was my little brother Nathan come back in this form, and carrying out his idee of helping folks. Yes, I had thought of it, and the doctor knew I had, and more'n a little, too. But it don't seem a satisfyin' sort of the'ry. Seems 's if folks, if they're let to come back at all, would come lookin' kind of different from us poor folks that's never had their opportunities ; they'd be more like angels or heavenly bein's, appears to me. But this man was just a real Bentley-lookin' kind of man, plain and homely, and dreadful bashful. Then if 'twas Nathan, why, he'd growed up. I wonder if they do grow up in that place. This man seemed just about as old as Nathan would have been if he'd lived. And he'd got the same idees as Nathan about helping folks and getting 'em out of trouble. And it was just me, his own sister, he helped. But then it don't stand to reason that a soul would come back to do such common kind of helping jobs as making a baby look pleasant to have its pictur' took, or fetching peppermint, or driving cows out of the corn, and all that. To be sure, it might come down to sing a favorite hymn to a dying woman, or to save a little child's life, but—no, I can't tell what I do think, and so I always tell Dr. Little.

"But," he says, in his solemn, book-word kind o' way that I've got by heart now—

"but, Mrs. Harris, do you consider this visitant a supernat'ral being? Do you call it a spirit or ghost?"

And I always answer, "No, Dr. Little, I don't dast to say I hold that."

"Well then, my dear Mrs. Harris," he says, again, "what do you call this apparition?"

And I always answer, "Why, I just call him a transient."

AUNT LIEFY

AUNT LIEFY

I DON'T know how it come about exactly ;
mebbe 'twas because I never rec'lected any
folks of my own. Or again, p'r'aps 'twas
owin' to the people where I lived not bein'
of the sociable sort. Or mebbe, likely 's not,
'twas all the fault of my own queer, cross-
grained, hard-to-get-along-with natur'. But
tennerate, there 'twas—a fact well known to
me and other folks, that I was the lonesomest
creatur' that ever lived. I hadn't a real
friend on the airth ; more'n that, I hadn't
scursely any acquaintances. Folks in the
village and town knew who I was, most of
'em, and I knew their names and some of
their faces ; but that was about all.

You asked me for just one partic'lar part
of my story, and I'm goin' to give it to you.
As for the rest, why, there's no call for me to

go into that now, and I ain't a-goin' to. How
I come to be there in Hilton, without any one
belongin' to me, or a soul in the whole world
; to set by me, or me to set by, why, all that's
another story, so we'll let it alone now. And
I'll begin just here, when I was a grown-up
woman, hard featur'd and harder natur'd, not
liked by anybody, and not havin', myself, a
mite of int'rest in any one on this airth or
outside of it. Never mind what I done for a
livin'; I got along. I had enough to eat and
drink, and clo'es to wear; and I wasn't beholden to anybody. I lived by myself in that
same little red house just out of the village
where you fust see me—the lonesomest creatur', as I said afore, that God ever made. My
whole name, you know, is Relief Staples; but
'twas years and years since I'd heard the fust
part. I was "Miss Staples" to the whole
town; and yet 'twasn't the kind of place
where they give folks sech names gen'rally.
Other single women of my age—old maids I
suppose you'd call 'em—was Ann Nichols, or
Lizzy Mount, or Hopey Palmer; and the
married ones was Aunt this or Aunty that
or Mother somebody. But I was allers "Miss

Staples" to man, woman, and child, speakin'
about me, or to me, no matter which. And,
queer enough, I never thought of myself by
any other name. I'd most forgot I was Relief at all; for I even signed my name—to a
bill or paper, I never writ a letter—R. Staples.

I don't seem to remember much about when
I was a girl. There was reasons that haven't
got anything to do with this story why I was
diff'ent from the other children. Strangers
that come along and die right in the public
roads, and leave young ones too little to know
their own names or where they come from,
can't expect their children to be fav'rites in
the c'mmunity, especially if they're put in
among the town-poor at fust. I know I got
some schoolin' at the little deestrict school
on the north road; but I don't rec'lect much
about the other children playin' with me, or
callin' me by my fust name, as they done one
'nother in the games, or in spellin' and read-
in'. I don't b'lieve I liked 'em much, or them
me; for after I growed up I allers had a dis-
like to young ones, and they returned it every
speck. Fact is, I can't remember likin' anything much in them days. I done my work

without takin' much notice of it; I eat my meals, sometimes one place, sometimes another, settin' or standin', or workin' about, as I felt like it. I went to bed and got up; that was my life. All my neighbors had posy gardens, and most of 'em had flowers in the house too; but I never thought of sech a thing. What was the use of it? I went to meetin' sometimes; because—well, I don't seem to rec'lect why I did go, but I did. But it didn't int'rest me, and I didn't take no great notice of what went on. That it meant much of anything to me, myself, never come into my head in those days.

I'm leavin' out, as I said afore, everything that hasn't really got to do with my story. So I needn't stop to tell you how it come about that I was trav'lin' one day—the day my story really begins—on a kind of business errand, over the Middle Railroad, nor how I come to get off at the wrong station; but there I was. I meant to go to Wellsville. I'd been there afore and knew how it looked; and the train hadn't hardly started after leavin' me before I see I was wrong. There wasn't any real depot, only a kind of platform to wait on, and there wasn't a soul in sight. I looked about a little, and then I begun to walk along the road, not carin' much what I did. My business wasn't pressin', 'twas the middle of the day and lots of daylight ahead, so I jest walked slowly along. The road was an uphill one, and no houses along it at fust. I rec'lect that, though I didn't notice much besides ; for up to that day, you know, I never did notice things. But that was the last of that way of livin', as you'll see pretty soon.

It was in the fall of the year, early in October, and, as I could tell from what come arterwards, the trees all along the way was red and yeller and bright-lookin', and I was steppin' on leaves colored the same way ; but I didn't seem to see 'em. I don't know how long or how fur I walked, or what I was thinkin' about. Somehow it don't seem as if I ever was thinkin' much about anything those times. Mebbe my mind run a little on that piece of business I was goin' to attend to, or some work I'd promised to do, I don't remember.

The fust thing that stands out, as I look back now, was hearin' a man speakin'. He was in a buggy; but I hadn't noticed the sound of wheels, and he was close up to me, comin' down the road facin' me, as if he was on the way to the station I'd come from, 'fore I see him. He drawed up right alongside of me. He was an oldish man, with a pleasant-lookin' kind of face, only a mite solemn and sorry like, and he says, " I'm so glad you've got here. They've waited, thinkin' you might be on this train. I'm goin' on to tell the minister, or I'd give you a lift ; but some one'll meet you." And then, 'fore I'd had time to say anything, he says, in a low sort of voice, "I'm dreadful sorry for you ; we all be." And then he started his horse and rode away. It seems odd now that I didn't wonder more about what he meant, or ask him somethin', or call after him that I guessed he'd made a mistake. But, if you'll believe me, all I could think of in that fust minute was that somebody was waitin' for me and expectin' me ; somebody was glad I'd come ; and, 'bove and over all, somebody was dreadful sorry for me. Not one of them things, 's fur 's I know, had ever happened to me afore, and though I made sure 'twas all a mistake, somehow jest for a minute I had the comfortablest feelin' I'd ever had in my life. Comfortable in my mind, I mean ; but queer enough, it made me feel weak in my body and with a kind of choked-up, swelly throat. I walked along, tryin' to think, when I see a carryall comin' down the road towards me, with a boy drivin'.

"Oh, there you be !" he says, as he stopped the old horse. "Get right in. They put off the funeral, you see, thinkin' you might get here on this noon-train."

I stood still in the road, lookin' at him ; but he says, "Hurry ! Pa told me to drive quick"; and I got in. I don't know what made me do it. I go over and over that day sometimes in my mind, and try to think how 'twas I fell in with everything so, without explainin' or askin' questions. The only way I can make it out reas'nable is, that I was so took up with this bein' expected and took notice of and made much on, that I jest let myself have the comfort of it all, without sayin' or doin' a thing that might 'a' stopped it. The boy didn't say much ; he driv fast, shakin' the reins and cluckin' to the horse. The road was pretty rough, and the wagon was shackly and shook about and rattled, and we couldn't 'a' held much talk even if we'd had a mind to. We met some folks, and they all looked at me in the same way, kind of int'rested and friendly, but allers sorry, real sorry — that was what struck me most.

"They've mistook me for somebody else," I says to myself; "but I can't help likin' it, and I won't tell 'em jest for a spell. It feels so good to be looked at that way. I'll wait a minute 'fore I tell 'em." Mebbe I didn't put it into jest them words, but I was thinkin' somethin' most like that, I know.

All of a sudden the boy whoaed his horse and stopped. I see a little gal in a red frock runnin' 'crost the road and holdin' up somethin'. She was all out of breath and her little face red, she'd run so; and she didn't say anythin', on'y reached up and put somethin' in my lap and run off. The boy whipped up, and we went on. I looked down into my lap and see some yeller posies.

"What be they?" I says, more to my own self than anything. But the boy, he says, in that kind of way boys does when they're sorry and most ashamed of bein', "Gold'nrod, ye know, that she set so much by."

Now that bloom grows all along the roads through our part of the country; but somehow I hadn't ever noticed it afore, and I never 'd heerd its name—not to rec'lect it. And whoever did he mean by "she"? But that give me a little more to hold on by. All this bein' sorry for me, and takin' care and all, had somethin' to do with this somebody he spoke of as "she." I begun to feel dreadful queer and choky, and 's if I must know right straight off all about her, and what had happened. It's a mistake, I says to myself, but oh, I jest can't let on that 'tis yet, and me to go back to bein' no account to anybody, and never wanted or expected anywheres again.

We kep' meetin' folks; but they all turned 's quick as they see us, and went back the way we was goin'. And I could hear teams comin' along behind us too.

Bime-by I see a little white house ahead and a good many men folks standin' round it. And the boy drawed up in front of that house. Two or three men came out to the carriage, plain, farmer-lookin' men, with kind of tanned, weather-beat faces, but all with the same sort of sorry look, and I see they was goin' to help me out. I'd jest been a goin' to tell 'em who I was and how 'twas all a mistake ; but for the life of me I couldn't then.

They'll find me out in a minute, I says to myself ; but I can't tell 'em now. For you see, in all my born days I hadn't ever afore been helped out of anything, and I wanted to see how 'twould seem. They done it real gentle ; and somehow they led me into the gate. All the men in the front yard, they stood back each side of the path while I walked up to the door. I hadn't more'n stepped over the sill into the entry, where 'twas sort of dark, when I felt somethin' queer, warm, and soft, and wrappy ; and I see I was in somebody's arms. 'Twas an old woman with white hair, and a soft, wrinkled face, and sech a mothery look all over her—I wonder how my mother looked ; and she put her face up again' mine, and I felt 'twas all wet. I don't believe I'd ever, afore that, felt anybody's tears, not even my own, sence I was a baby.

She'll say somethin' now, I thinks to my-

self, that'll show me where the mistake is;
and then 'twill all come out, and I'll jest go
back. But she didn't say but one thing, after
all, and that didn't help. "Oh, my dear, my
dear!" she says. That was all.

You can't blame me for not tellin' then,
not jest then, can you? S'pose you hadn't
ever in all your hull life been called "my
dear"; and you was all kind of shakin' and
chokin' and cry'ey, and glad and sorry to once
with hearin' it, could you go and spile it right
straight off by ownin' up you hadn't no claim
to it? Well, I couldn't, anyway.

She took me into a little bedroom and put
me in a chair. She said there was plenty of
time for me to rest a spell; for folks had got
to be let know I was come, and that the
fun'ral could go on. She untied my bunnet-
strings and unpinned my shawl. She done
a lot of things to me that I didn't hardly
know what was, they was so new and queer
to me, not bein' used to 'em, you know. She
talked a good deal; but I didn't take much
notice of the words, I was so took up with
her softly voice and the things she was doin'
to me. But I know she kep' sayin' over 'n'

over, "If you could only 'a' got here afore
she went! If you could only 'a' got here !"

I tried to say somethin'; but some ways
my throat was all dry, and 'fore I could get
out any words, she says, "Oh, I know you
couldn't, you poor dear creatur', and she
knew it too. She wanted you dreadful bad,"
she says, the tears a runnin' down her pretty, old, wrinkled face; "but she knew you
couldn't get here, and most the very last
word she spoke was your name, my dear."

Well, that finished me. Up to that time I
hadn't cried any myself. I don't b'lieve I
knew how, exactly, never havin' done it sence
I was a baby. But now I found the water
fallin' out o' my eyes like rain. Mebbe 'twas
because I knew 'twas all a mistake; mebbe
again owin' to my half-believin' 'twas real and
true after all, and somebody was layin' dead
that had set by me so that she'd wanted me
dreadful, and said over my name with her
last breath most. Anyway I cried and cried
and cried. I'd 'a' said afore that, if anybody 'd
asked me, that it must hurt to cry, that I
shouldn't like it; but—I did. It seemed to
help me, and rest me, and comfort me, to

make me diff'ent from what I'd ever been
afore in all my life—more like other folks,
and jest a little mite like the white-haired
old woman and the people outside with that
sorry look on their featur's.

I don't know how long 'twas, mebbe only a
few minutes, mebbe more, but arter a spell,
anyway, we went out o' that little bedroom
and into the settin'-room. It was shet up
and dark like, and I couldn't see much at fust.
They put me into a seat, and pretty soon I
found there was lots of folks round me.
There was chairs in rows, and people in 'em ;
and there was a somethin', black and strange,
covered and shet up and still, and I knew,
without bein' told, that she they'd said had
wanted me, and set by me, and spoke about
me up to the very last, was layin' there. My
old woman was settin' close by me, and when
she see my eyes fixed on that, she says in a
whisper, "I wish you could 'a' seen her, she
was so peaceful and pleasant - lookin' and
nat'ral. But you know how 'twas, and that we
couldn't wait."

So I wasn't goin' to see her even this way !
I shouldn't ever know how she looked, livin'

or dead. Well, I wasn't exactly sorry. I most dreaded the idee of seein' her, for fear somehow I might be disapp'inted. For I'd got a'ready a notion of my own about her, from what the dear old woman told me, and things I heerd whispered round as we set waitin'.

Then somebody says, " Here's the minister," and an old man come up to me. I looked up at him ; I hadn't ever seen jest sech a face afore, or if I had, it hadn't made much impression on me. 'Twasn't exactly sorry, but 's if it had been over 'n over again, and knew all about it ; and there was a look as if he was hopin' somethin' real hard, and lottin' on gettin' it too—a kind of shinin' in his eyes and a still sort of look jest round his mouth. He took hold of my hand, and he said somethin'. It don't seem as if I heerd the words, each one on 'em ; but I gathered lots o' meanin' out of it somehow, and I knew that he was dreadful sorry for me, but glad enough for her, though I couldn't hardly see why jest then, and I see too that he knew I was goin' to be glad too, some day.

Well, the fun'ral begun and went on. I disremember whether or no I'd ever been to a fun'ral afore; but I'd seen 'em go by, of course, and thought I knew all about 'em. But this wasn't a bit like what I'd conceited. I can't tell you jest how 'twas diff'ent; mebbe one thing was I was diff'ent, even in that short spell. Things the minister read or spoke, though I'd heerd some of 'em afore in meetin' and elsewheres, got to meanin' somethin' now when I was listenin' so close to find out somethin' about her that laid there, and whether there was any chance of my seein' her some day. And when he prayed—well, I'd seen folks pray, time and again, but didn't think of its meanin' much of anythin'; and as for prayin' myself, I didn't s'pose I knew how. P'r'aps I didn't, and wa'n't prayin' then; but I was secondin' ev'ry single thing the old minister said, and hopin' with all my heart and mind and body they'd come true. Ain't that a kind of prayin'? And somebody else said somethin'; and they sung things softly, and prayed again. And in ev'ry single thing I could see they thought she that laid there b'longed to me more'n to anybody else and that I was the sorriest of any one there.

They prayed for me more'n all the rest; they talked about me, not by name, but "our sister," they says, "her that's so sorely afflict- ed," "she that was so closely bound up with her that's gone," and things like that. Oh, I can't begin to tell you what 'twas to me to be, for the fust time in all my days, right in the middle of things, 'stead of alone outside ; with folks all lovin' me and bein' sorry for me and askin' for things to happen to me. I couldn't, I jest couldn't, put a stop to it all by ownin' up 'twas a mistake somehow.

And then we went to the little buryin'- ground. 'Twas close by, and folks walked ; and I was ahead of all, and closest to her. I can see it all so plain, for I b'lieve 'twas the fust out-o'-doors thing I'd ever really looked at—in a takin'-notice way, I mean. The trees —there was a lot of 'em round—was all bright and gay-lookin' with their red and yeller and browny leaves, and the sky was all blue with little white clouds strimmered over it. There was ever so many posies growin' in the paths, gold'nrod — I'd learnt that name a'ready — and purple blooms mixed in with 'em, and the air was full of a minty, spicy sort o' smell from yarbs in the grass. And up in a tree, jest over the place they'd dug her grave, set a little bird a-singin' 's loud and sweet 's he could sing.

Then the minister said some words—sing'lar, wonderful sort o' words they 'peared to me then, in fact they do now—and they laid her down there. And the sun was a-shinin'; there was a bumble - bee buzzin' about the posies, and a butterfly lightin' on 'em. And up in the maple, 'mongst the red leaves, that little bird was singin' with all his might and main. There was some tears, o' course; but folks kep' smilin' through 'em till they was more like rainbows.

Why, thinks I to myself, 'tain't like a fun'ral one bit; it's more like plantin' a flower.

And then they all come round me, jest me; the women, the men, the children, and ev'ry one had somethin' to say about her that was gone, and what she'd been to 'em all, what she was to me and me to her. There was an old blind man she'd took care of and read to, and some little orphan children she'd mothered and done for; and there was friends she'd been friend to, and meetin'-folks she'd

worked with in doin' good, and—all of a sudden it all come over me what she must 'a' been
and how I'd heerd of her too late ; and then
I thought o' my lonesome, dried-up, good-for-
nothin' life all ahind me, and how diff'ent
'twould 'a' been if she'd really b'longed to
me, as these folks all thought she done, and
seemed 's if I couldn't bear it. Sech a sorrer
and longin' and mournin' and grief come
rollin' over me, like waves o' the sea, and I
see I'd never had any real trouble or grief or
loss afore in my life. Oh, what was it for ?
What did it mean ? How was I goin' to bear
it, anyhow ?

They see I was givin' way, and one after
'nother begun to tell me things she'd said
about me, word she'd sent to me. "She said
she'd be watchin' for you till you come," says
one, most in a whisper. "She told me," says
another, "to tell you not to feel bad you
couldn't get here to take care of her, 'For,'
says she, 'if you'll on'y take care o' somebody else that's sick or lonesome 'twill be jest
the same 's doin' it for me.'" And a little
gal, with yeller curls and sech a soft face,
reached up, and says, in the littlest whisper,

"She told me to give you this." And she kissed me. I never 'd been kissed afore.

And then the old minister, he kind of drawed me to one side and he says, "She asked me over and over, afore she died, to tell you this, that she forgive you everythin', if there was anythin' to forgive, and that you mustn't mourn and fret thinkin' mebbe you was one cause of her dyin'; for even if you was, she was glad, and more'n glad, to lay down her life for you."

I can't hardly rec'lect how I got away from 'em all, and from that grave and the little buryin'-ground, and found my way back to the station. I on'y know I didn't tell 'em 't all 'twas a mistake, but come away without ownin' up anythin'. I took the cars back to Hilton. I see so many things out of the winder I hadn't took notice of that mornin'. There was gold'nrod all 'longside the way— her fav'rite flower; with the sun a-shinin' on it and the cars goin' by so quick it made the roads look like the golden streets the minister 'd talked about. And I see little buryin'-grounds with green graves and white stones that made me think of where she was layin'.

And when we stopped, sometimes I'd hear a
bird like that one up in the maple-tree.
There was a little gal in the car with yeller
curls, like the one that kissed me, and I found
myself a-smilin' at her, and she smiled back
to me.

And when I got out at my station and was
walkin' up the village street to the red house,
things looked diff'ent from what they ever
done afore. I see I was walkin' on red and
yeller leaves that looked pretty and made a
rustlin' sort of noise as I stepped on 'em,
jest 's they done 's I stood in the little buryin'-ground where we laid her. And there
was little white houses along the street, somethin' like the one where I'd been, and where
I s'pose she'd lived ; and I begun to wonder
if there was anybody resemblin' her livin' in
these. I never 'd wondered much about folks
afore, didn't take any int'rest in 'em.

And jest 'fore I got to my house I see a
woman comin'. She had a black dress on,
and 's I looked at her I rec'lected she was a
neighbor o' mine, and that I'd heerd she'd
lost her on'y child, a little boy, a spell back.
All of a sudden I 'peared to know what that

meant, and see the coffin, and him a-layin' in it, and the folks all together, and heerd the minister's voice sayin' them wonderful words; and 'fore I knew what I was doin' I held out my hand to her and I heerd my own voice a-sayin', "I'm dreadful sorry for you."

She looked into my face 's if she hadn't ever see it afore—I s'pose it looked diff'ent somehow, with my eyes all swelly and red—and she says, with the tears a-comin fast, "Thank ye, thank ye! I see you've met with a loss yourself, Miss Staples, and that makes you feel for me."

I wa'n't tellin' a lie, was I, when I says, "I have, I have, and I do feel for you?" For I had lost all I ever had in my hull life, and jest 's quick 's I knew I had it, too.

Now, 'tisn't scurcely the thing for me to tell the rest ; I don't hardly know how to say it. You asked me to tell you how 'twas I changed about so, as folks told you I done—from a lonesome, unfeelin', unreligious woman, not havin' a mite of int'rest in anybody, nor them havin' any in me, to somethin' diff'ent. And I've told you all I know about what fetched about the change.

I never knew anythin' more about that fun'ral, nor the one we buried that day, nor what I was to her nor her to me. , I was afraid to find out, so I never asked any questions, nor went back to that station, nor looked in the papers to see who was dead there. As long 's I didn't really know the partic'lars, nor who they took me for, and why they took me for her, why, there wasn't any harm, was there, in my feelin' she was mine now, let alone what she'd been afore ; that that was my grave to think on and mourn over, and, what's more, hope about ? Tennerate, I done it ; and small credit to me that it fetched me some good, and made me alter my old, hateful ways. For it stands to reas'n that havin' a sorrer myself—and 'twas one, though mebbe you can't see how—made me notice other folks's troubles and feel for 'em and try to help 'em, as I was helped.

And hearin' what she liked and set by, posies and sech, made me begin to notice and get fond on 'em myself. And that's how my gardin got to what 'twas when you fust see it, and my winders and porch so chock full of growin' things. And of course you see now how I took to feedin' them birds that you was so struck with, comin' round the steps and pickin' up my crumbs and seeds, lightin' on me, and all that; that was owin', you see, to that little bird a-singin' in the red maple over her grave. I never forgot him, the peart little fellow, singin' and singin' away with all his might and main 's if he knew somethin' good was goin' to happen. And them queer folks you used to watch a-comin' in my gate and hangin' round there—old lame Jesse and foolish Nance and that little rickety Dan with the hump on his poor little back—why, I had them come, and done for 'em, on'y jest 'cause she done that kind of thing, they said. 'Twa'n't nothin' 'riginal on my part, that wa'n't—jest copyin' her, you see.

That was why I took to nussin' the sick and all that; and that's how they come to take to callin' me Aunt Relief, and then Aunt Liefy, 'stead o' Miss Staples.

The other part—'tain't for me to say a word about that; Some One else done it, if 'tis done. It's reas'nable, ain't it, that I should take some kind of int'rest in what made this friend

of mine I hadn't ever see the sort of person
they made her out, and that I should study up
about that, and about those sing'lar words
the minister used at the fun'ral, and about
the place where she'd gone to, and, 'bove and
over all, what chance there was of my gettin'
to see her after a spell. And findin' out con-
cernin' all them things, why, of course I found
out more'n I was lookin' for. You see, the
one thing that had worked on me most that
day was hearin' she'd forgive me things; for
I hadn't ever been forgive anythin' in my
hull life—not to know it, I mean. And somehow I didn't dwell on that part about my
havin' done anythin' to bring about her death,
as much 's I did on what she said about bein'
glad and more'n glad to lay down her life
for me. That was the one thing I guess I
thought of most, comin' home that day from
her buryin' and arterwards. Any one that
set by me enough to be glad to lay their life
down on my account, it seemed too sing'lar
to take in, and 's if it couldn't act'lly be.
Well, it don't seem a mite less sing'lar now;
but I've found it could act'lly be!

So I'm jest a-goin' on all the time now as

if I'd had folks. It's most 's if I'd had, you see. I've got a grave, anyhow, in a little, sweet, minty, spicy-smellin' buryin'-ground full o' posies, gold'nrod, and sech; and I've got messages some one left for me—word she sent—and I'm follerin' 'em and doin' 'em 's well 's I can. And I've been once in my life to a fun'ral that was more to me than to any one else there, where I was prayed for and comforted and pitied and set by. It's most 's if I'd had folks, don't you think so? That's what I hold.

And I don't see how I done anybody any harm by not tellin' 'twas all a mistake and I was took for somebody else. If I was, why, I guess the right one got along a spell arterwards and got the same comfort out of it I did, and mebbe more. So 't didn't hurt her.

And there's one thing can't be took from me. There was somebody lay there that day, whether she was anythin' to me afore all that or not; and I know what she'd been, from what folks said about her; and I know where she's gone, from what she was and b'lieved and said. So there ain't no manner o' harm, and you can't make me think there is, in my lookin' forrard to seein' her one of these days, and pretty soon now. And when I do see her, why, I sha'n't have to go into a long explainin' and showin' how it come about, and why I didn't own up that day she was buried. She'll see it in a minute, if she ain't seen it a'ready ; and that if I ain't that one she'd set by so long and that had set by her, I'm the one that's jest lived for her ever sence, and tried to copy her and act like her, and love the ones she loved, and do for the ones she done for, and, partic'lar, that's tried to get herself ready and fit to be let in to see her some day.

And I know cert'in sure that there's Some One else up there that 'll understand all about it too, without my tellin ; and He'll know what 'twas to me to think of a buryin'-spot filled with sweet spices, in a place like a gardin o' posies, and of some one layin' there for a spell —some one that had set by me so much that she'd 'a' been glad and more'n glad to lay down her life for me.

THE END

By JAMES LANE ALLEN

A KENTUCKY CARDINAL. Illustrated by ALBERT E. STERNER. Square 32mo, Cloth, Ornamental, $1 00; Half Calf, $2 00.

The portrayal of nature alone would give the book high rank, but the story sets the poem to music.—*Chicago Times.*

AFTERMATH. Part Second of "A Kentucky Cardinal." Square 32mo, Cloth, Ornamental, $1 00; Half Calf, $2 00.

A slender stream of tender and delicate imagining, filtered through prose which is almost poetry.—*New York Observer.*

FLUTE AND VIOLIN, and Other Kentucky Tales and Romances. Illustrated. Post 8vo, Cloth, Ornamental, $1 50; Silk Binding, $2 25.

The stories of this volume are fiction of high artistic value—fiction to be read and remembered as something rare, fine, and deeply touching.—*New York Independent.*

THE BLUE-GRASS REGION OF KENTUCKY, and Other Kentucky Articles. Illustrated. 8vo, Cloth, $2 50.

We are indebted to Mr. James Lane Allen for the first adequate treatment of an interesting subject—adequate both in respect of knowledge and of literary skill—in the book entitled "The Blue-Grass Region of Kentucky."—*New York Sun.*

PUBLISHED BY HARPER & BROTHERS, NEW YORK

☞ *The above works are for sale by all booksellers, or will be sent by the publishers by mail, postage prepaid, on receipt of the price.*

By REBECCA HARDING DAVIS

FRANCES WALDEAUX. A Novel. Illustrated by T.
DE THULSTRUP. Post 8vo, Cloth, Ornamental, $1 25.

A capital novel, of the modern, vivacious type. . . . The mi-
nor characters of the story furnish no stint of witty interplay,
as they sojourn through Europe, and the keen thrusts and cap-
tious hits at the European nobility and American ambitions
make truly racy reading.—*Boston Transcript.*

It grows in interest from chapter to chapter, and retains its
grasp on the absorbed attention from beginning to end. This
ought to prove one of the most successful stories of the year.—
Philadelphia Press.

"Frances Waldeaux" shows admirable literary reticence and
good character drawing. The author never reveals her plot pre-
maturely, and the book therefore holds the interest to the last.
And she makes living beings of her characters.—*Chicago
Tribune.*

DOCTOR WARRICK'S DAUGHTERS. A Novel. Illustrated by CLIFFORD CARLETON. Post 8vo, Cloth,
Ornamental, $1 50.

A very enjoyable story, . . . written in a sprightly tone, with
here and there a touch of delightfully amiable banter. . . . The
characters are strong and drawn effectively.—*Independent*, N.Y.

A story of unusual merit. Its success is in its plot, though
its descriptions and its characters are handled with a firm and
intelligent grasp.—*Boston Journal.*

A thoroughly interesting story; more than that, an absorb-
ing one. There is a real vitality about the characters and the
situations that fascinates one.—*Living Church*, Chicago.

The reader will be at once struck with the freshness of the
author's theme and of her method. . . . One of the best novels
of the day.—*Philadelphia Inquirer.*

NEW YORK AND LONDON

HARPER & BROTHERS, PUBLISHERS

www.ingramcontent.com/pod-product-compliance
Lightning Source LLC
Chambersburg PA
CBHW030114030726
47498CB00007B/2381